Remedy

Return to The Old World

By:

J.Z. El-azar

The characters and events portrayed in this book are fictional. Any similarity to real persons, living or dead, is coincidental and not intended by the author.

Hardcover ISBN:979-8-9918855-5-3

Paperback ISBN:979-8-9918855-4-6

E Book ISBN: 979-8-9918855-3-9

Cover Art by: Magi Purnomo

Illustrations by: Aurelia Inskeep

Other illustrations by: Akar Studios

Library of Congress

United States Of America

To My Family............

For all the lessons you learned, Will be the lessons I teach. To the best support system in the world, I love you.

Table of Contents

Chapter 1:

Replanning

The winds are blowing at a high speed on this shady afternoon. Things in the world have not been the same lately. Death numbers have gone up in a matter of months; population is decreasing to the point where animals are being affected. World leaders have set up meetings to discuss what they can do in this crisis. But it is not enough for them to move forward with a plan. Theodore seems like the only man in the world, who holds the key to solving this worldwide crisis. As tensions rise within different countries, states, and cities. Crime rates also rise across the globe; people grow impatient waiting for the government to act. Conspiracies and myths even begin to surface; people are starting to believe that this disease is a manufactured disease. People are saying that the disease was created to start a New World. Like a reset of some kind and hell, you can't blame people for thinking this way, especially now, when nothing is being done to help anyone. Protesters have gone on a rampage in front of hospitals, to the point where hospitals now have at least a police precinct within their property. Others have also gone to social media and start theories, to as why they believe this disease is man made. The President hasn't made a speech in two weeks; other world leaders have not spoken in at least a month or so. Supposedly, Central America and Africa are on the verge to the population dropping to zero. England, where the Eyidrotheria disease started is on a mass quarantine. Japan is also on a mass quarantine, where only a quarter of the city is holding off those who aren't infected. Russia on the other hand has not suffered such loses, people believe is due to the wintry weather over there. The Environment looks horrible, trees are dying, animals are suffering, due to the lack of human inactivity. The hospitals have had more deaths in the last six months. Majority of the time, if a birth happens, the babies won't last more than a week unless they are put in an incubator right away. But even then, they will have to be fed and raised through the incubator until a cure is found. But the cure is found, in fact, the cure has been discovered after World War Three. The only people that know about this cure are The Four Scientists that have fled from Theodore, along with James Matthews, who is now deceased, due to a gunshot to the head in the hands of Sergeant Thaddeus Luther the third. Besides Spike, the hybrids whose blood holds the cure are believed to be unaware of this discovery. Theodore, who also holds the answers to saving thousands of lives worldwide, who for unknown reasons has not announced anything to the world. Or what about even Sergeant Luther who we just mentioned and who allies himself with Madman Theodore, every one of these people has one thing in common. They are all selfish, selfish enough to let people, animals and babies die. With one group living on an island with the cure itself and the other two men just sitting back and watching the world decay in front of their eyes. These people all share something in common and that is being selfish. Whether they keep the cure for their own entertainment in watching the world suffer or whether they are afraid to announce the cure. But what about even the hybrids themselves? The ones who know they hold the cure. Are they to blame? But again, the hybrids can't be blamed, hell the scientists can't be blamed either. Again, these scientists and hybrids are far away from any civilization, to even know what is going on out there in the world. Out there, where people are suffering, animals are dying. The only way to know is by the environment around them. But even if the hybrids and scientists find out what's happening in the world out there, what will they do next? Will they continue to live on their lives on this island in fear? Or will fear become the new way to avoid everything? But, just maybe in hope that they put fear to the side and selfishness is not in their nature. Just maybe, this will bring the hope we need back, A hope that just maybe, the remedy, the cure, can be brought back to the to The Old World.

Chapter 2:

Team AdreNaline

Joanne Wright is a middle-aged woman of a mixed background who works for the FBI. Joanne or Joanna wears seeing glasses, she is tan colored with short black hair and a slim body type. Her inspiration in her career, came from her father Frederick Wright an African American man who was a top CIA agent himself. Joanne's mother was of a Latin background from Puerto Rico who also worked for the CIA as a dispatcher, which is how both Joannes parents met. Joanna is part of an FBI team that now only consists of herself, a hacker by the nickname "The Jester", her love interest who goes by the name Reginald "The Eye" Cooper, he is a white American man in his late Thirties. He is six two, well-trimmed beard and uses a slick back hair style with chestnut brown eyes. Alongside, they also have an investigator named Wallace "The Zombie" Terrence, who is a White

Caucasian heavyset man in his late forties. The fifth member was a man named Raymond Styke who is no longer with the crew, due to unknown reasons. No one knows if he is still alive or deceased, he was going on a solo mission which he informed his team and that was the last he was heard of. Joanne and Raymond were the regulars in field operations, which means they would go on enemy territory of any site and either fight or investigate. Wallace acts as a spy, to either what they are investigating or whom, if he must... he will go undercover on whatever or whoever it is the FBI finds threatening. Reginald oversees drones and is well known for his sniping skills around the country, which hence, why he has the nickname "The Eye." Reginald needs a hacker to access the country's drone and cameras which is where "The Jester" comes in. The Jester as mentioned before is the hacker.

His real name is Larry Simmons, he is in his mid-thirties, likes to wear red, he is at least six feet tall with a buzz cut and seeing glasses, he has on his face a big mustache, which the team poke fun of. This group of people are known by the FBI as team AdreNaline with the "N" in adrenaline being capital. This team, being FBI, has been involved in controversial missions before and has had their share in battles as well. So, what is it that makes this team so important? Well, a discovery has been made in Straton City, law enforcement have discovered James Matthews old warehouse that was located by the pier. In the warehouse, law enforcement found wired skeletal hands and different samples of the Eyidrotheria disease. The city has called law enforcement; law enforcement then calls the FBI. Due to reasons of the government believing one of their own is involved with making a manufactured disease. The CIA is also aware but only interact when the problem is threatening towards the president. The FBI believes in the disease being part of something bigger and more threatening, which is why they even considered this team. The Eye, Larry, takes the phone call and the mission, which is simple, extract the items found in James's warehouse lab and bring them in for examination. The other, is to find out why there are samples of the Eyidrotheria disease and investigate the metal skeletal hands in plain view. This reason is why Team AdreNaline has been sent to investigate and discover why James's warehouse lab has so much information that the government themselves do not. As the team begins to work on the mission Reginald speaks.

"Alright team, Joanne, and I will go in to investigate, Wallace you will act out as a police officer of Straton City. Make sure to keep any type of civilian far away as possible, do not let them inside, no cameras... nothing. We shouldn't have a problem with civilians, sadly the street and neighborhood the warehouse is located on is a ghost town, thanks to none other than the Eyidrotheria but, just keep an eye out. The Chief of police says he's waiting for us to arrive, so for now, the city police are holding off the perimeter; just in case the media somehow gets a hold of this information. Once the chief assures me that paparazzi, journalists, and any news team aren't present, the street will be ours. That means no one and I mean no one is allowed anywhere near that street. We have gained access ourselves and even have the whole area blocked off. It is a warehouse located in a quiet street near the pier. We can't have any word of this out to the world yet."

Everyone agrees with the plan.

The Jester speaks. "Any information on a computer or database in that warehouse bring it to me."

Reginald laughs. "Of course, brother, you got it."

Jester smirks sarcastically and continues eating his peanuts.

"Alright let's head out!" Says Reggie.

The team take off in a boat from the location of an abandoned air base near an abandoned dock. As the boat speeds through the water's surface, Joanne goes to the front of the boat where she lets the high wind hit her face gently as she tells herself. "Hopefully this helps us get some answers, we sure as hell need it."

Chapter 3:

Discovering

Joanna begins to narrate as Team AdreNaline arrives in Straton City. She begins by saying.

"We all arrived in the nearby pier to the city. Someone was shot and killed a couple of days before, which led the police officers of Straton City to investigate the premises. Upon doing so, the victim's yacht was stolen according to the victim's family. The family told law enforcement, that the victim goes out on the boat during Father's Day. As detectives began to investigate, they noticed that the bullet belonged to none other than James Matthews, a contractor who made house calls for a couple of people in the city and even did some construction work.

Matthews was not present in his stay, but one of his clients gave the police a tip of a warehouse he bought by the docks. Detectives investigated the warehouse and once they discovered what was inside, they called the FBI. I, Reggie, and Wallace approached the front of the warehouse. There, a Detective told us the investigation was ours and we proceeded to look around. First thing I noticed was bionic hands all over the place, including what looked like a lab table. We also noticed a fridge, which inside contained a capsule of the Eyidrotheria disease and another capsule that said SPIKES DNA. Reggie looked over at the capsule and gave me a look, so I can observe it through a telescope."

Reggie says to Joanne while she is looking at Spikes DNA. "What do you see?"

Joanna replies. "Nothing special but it does look different from any other DNA or blood sample."

Reggie asks. "You want to mix that with the Eyidrotheria sample just out of curiosity?"

Joanne nods her head, and Reggie carefully brings Joanne the Sample of the Eyidrotheria. Joanne puts a drop of Spikes DNA on the Eyidrotheria using a water dropper. As she watches through her telescope, she sees the DNA is taking over the Eyidrotheria to what seems, to be destroying the disease.

Joanna looks at Reggie in shock as she screams out loud. "My god we found the cure!"

Reggie calms her down as he looks around. Joanne tells Reggie to look for himself, which he does, and he replies as well.

"My God.... We... we need to take this information to headquarters now!"

As the two stare at each other in happiness, a voice in the earpiece interrupts.

"Looks like we've got company they just entered the perimeter from the street." The Jester says.

Just outside by the back of James warehouse a black Suburban pulls up with dark tints. Three men step out dressed in all black with ski masks on, behind the three men is none other than Sergeant Luther who is also dressed in black and wears an eyepatch. Wallace is still patrolling the front as an undercover police officer. Wallace is wearing an earpiece when he hears the Jester. The Jester sits by in a black minivan, watching all the cameras through the screens inside the van. There, The Jester sees the three men about to surround Wallace.

The Jester quickly says. "Wallace, you got threat one on your left and two to the right!"

Joanne and Reggie hear this as well and pack up Spikes DNA in a briefcase and head out to help Wallace. The Jester hops out the van with a gun in his hand and heads towards the front of the warehouse where Wallace stands. Wallace runs towards his left to take care of the one threat, but as soon as he turns the corner no one is there. Joanne and Reggie head to the exit of the warehouse, where they are stopped by the sounds of assault rifles hitting through the window. Wallace hears the shots and heads over to the front where he was before. But as soon as he turns the corner Sergeant Luther punches Wallace in the throat. Wallace holds his throat while coughing and he falls on his back.

Sergeant Luther stands over the body wearing black gloves pointing a silencer at Wallace, he shoots Wallace three times, hitting Wallace in the chest, neck, and chin.

Meanwhile The Jester runs towards the two shooters who are still shooting at the warehouse. But then, The Jester gets shot at by the third masked man towards his right side. The Jester hides behind a bus stop made of metal, he begins to fire back at the Gunman.

Meanwhile inside Joanne and Reggie take cover as rounds and rounds of assault rifles are being unloaded.

Reggie looks at Joanne and speaks. "I found these little metal spheres; they look like grenades. I am going to click the button, throw, and see what happens!" Joanne nods.

Reggie throws the metal balls towards the front door, and it explodes letting out shards of metal and led. The two men outside scream in pain and the gunshots grow quiet, the two men are screaming in agony on the sidewalk floor. One is holding his face, which is full of metal shards like a bad case of acne, the other is holding his eyes with blood coming out of his eye sockets. With this perfect opportunity, Joanne and Reggie make their way to the front door to escape.

Chapter 4:

See No Evil, Hear No Evil

Joanne and Reggie head to the front of the warehouse. The two shooters scream in pain, as shards of metal stick to their face and skin. Joanne hears a gunshot from the left and sees the other shooter that was firing at The Jester. She can see the shooter and the Jester having a shootout. Reggie draws his gun at the shooter but, as soon as he is about to shoot, Luther kicks Reggie in the arm.

Reggie hits Luther with the briefcase and tackles Luther who is twice his size, both men wrestle on the sidewalk, Reggie elbows Luther while on top of him. Reggie then begins to crawl towards the left side of the building. Luther stands up and walks over to Reggie and Joanne, pulling his gun out shooting at the two.

Reggie grabs Joanne and says to her. “Take the DNA now! I’ll distract them, I got you covered."

Joanne looks at Reggie nods her head and runs off quickly. Reggie then pops out of the side of the building, shooting back at Luther with the gun he picked up while he was crawling. Luther Ducks down behind a postal service mailbox. As he shoots back at Reggie, Luther notices Joanne running towards the minivan. Luther whistles loud and the other shooter who was firing at the Jester chases Joanne. Reggie notices and immediately tries to go after the shooter. Luther shoots again this time hitting Reggie in the leg. Luther walks up to Reggie and points his gun at an injured Reggie. Then, the Jester starts firing shots at Sergeant Luther.

Luther takes cover and runs towards the back of the warehouse building. As Luther heads towards his suburban, he opens the back of the SUV and takes out bottles of gasoline. Luther lights two of them on fire and throws them through the warehouse's windows from the backside. Back in the front of the warehouse Joanne makes it to the minivan and takes off.

The shooter gets on a radio and signals the sergeant. "Sir the girl! She is heading East towards the docks!"

Sergeant Luther replies on his radio. "Get rid of the evidence! No survivors!"

The shooter walks over to the other two shooters screaming in pain and shoots both in the head. He sees Reggie and the Jester and as soon as he walks towards them a gunshot goes off and hits the shooter on the side of the neck. Both Reggie and the Jester look over and see Wallace on the ground pointing his gun at the shooter. The Jester helps Reggie up as they both limp towards Wallace. Wallace is holding his neck and suffocating in his own blood.

Reggie leans over and says to Wallace. "Hang on brother! Hang on!"

Wallace looks at Reggie and the Jester, Wallace smiles and stops breathing, his hands fall lifeless to the side of him, hitting the sidewalk. Reggie puts his head down in sadness and closes Wallace's eyes with his two fingers, as he does so, he sees the black suburban heading straight towards Joanne.

Reggie screams out. "Joanne! We must help Joanne!"

But with the streets being empty and the warehouse on fire there are no cars around. The Jester points at one of the dummy squad cars on the side of a building and both men limp towards the vehicle. Joanne drives at least sixty-five miles per hour on a neighborhood street, but the sergeant is right behind her. Joanne has no choice but to take the minivan straight to the dock and into the boat the team arrived on. Joanne drives into the dock, but the sergeant is shooting at her from behind.

The sergeant hits one of the back tires and the minivan loses control as it flips on the docks. The minivan rolls over at its driver's side, pinning Joanne's door against the dock floor. Luther hops off the suburban, walks over and sees Joanne struggling to get out the minivan. He watches her from the passenger side window. Joanne looks at the sergeant he smiles and shoots Joanne twice in the chest. Joanne falls back against her driver seat as the sergeant reaches down and grabs the briefcase, he hops back in his Suburban and takes off with only the sounds of his tires spinning through the empty streets.

About a couple of seconds later Reggie and The Jester pull up in the squad car to see the minivan flipped on its side. Reggie runs towards the vehicle and sees Joanne bleeding from her mouth. Reggie opens the passenger door that Is not pinned against the dock floor and carries Joanne out with the help of the Jester.

Reggie places Joanne on the dock and begins to sob. "Baby, baby listen to me you are going to be fine, ok? Just breathe slowly we're going to get you help right now."

Joanne struggles to talk as she begins to breathe fast, and tears run down her face.

Reggie says to her. "Baby, baby shhhh, it's ok it's ok don't speak just hang on."

Joanne looks at Reggie and stops breathing, her eyes wide open stare lifelessly back at Reggie. Reggie stops sobbing for a second, the Jester puts his head down and Reggie breaks down hysterically Both men stay with Joanne's body who in her mind she still says.

"I have never felt so cold in my life, I feel tired, and I want to talk to Reggie, but I cannot speak. I am dying, I am dying." Joanne says in her mind as her body turns cold and her hand falls lifeless to her right side.

Chapter 5:

Haven

Three years have passed since the hybrids made Sergeant Luther flee the island. For many reasons, the hybrids along with Shannon, Henry, Ryan, and Stacey migrated to another island. Using the boat James left behind and the weapons brought by the soldier hybrids, the island was ready for a war. Einsberg was aware of another island that only he would do wildlife testing on. This island was also filled with coconut trees, more land and space. Once the Sergeant was ran out of the island, the best thing to do is relocate. Einsberg had to drive the boat in three trips to relocate. As for the weapons, they are to stay on the boat unless the Sergeant and Theodore decide to attack. On this island, 656 is in a hut where he talks to himself as he explains the strange dreams he has been having.

656 says. "For as long as I can remember, my nightmares get worse every time. It is always the same, I see myself in a wide capsule full of water. Nothing in the dream changes but I always end up drowning and wake up. Lately, it seems like I am losing my breath more every time I wake up. It could be the age, or I am just losing my god damn mind. In my nightmares I always see this gate before I enter the capsule and see number. "Gate 2-B." strange, but for some reason I felt like I have been there before."

656 wakes up and sits at the edge of his bed. Next to him lays 598, who we see is impregnated and goes by the name. "Luna." As mentioned before, after three years a-lot has happened since Sergeant Luther fled the Island. Even with the island being bigger, the food source became incredibly low. Many because of the addition of hybrids, Three years ago. Some of these thoughts have caused a little tension within the island. Some males have become more territorial due to the women and food sources. It is not like before when everyone was working together to gather food. No, this is much different, even hybrids panic, panic causes worry, and worry causes anxiety. Just like normal human beings, this can drive any group to go mad or get hostile out of frustration. Janjii still being the chief, is seen with Maxayus walking through the side beach of the island. It is early morning and the winds are blowing heavily on this shady day. Janjii picks up sand in his hand and begins to run the sand through his palms.

Janjii takes a deep breath, he says to Maxayus. "Something is not right my son."

Maxayus raises his eyebrow in confusion, while holding a spear in his hand.

Maxayus responds. "Father, you have been saying this for months now what is it are we running out of food?"

Janjii nods his head, closes his eyes, and breathes the windy air. Janjii says. "The earth my son, the earth. It does not feel the same as before. I am starting to believe our food sources have not decreased due to our population, but rather than our fish and trees dying."

Maxayus looks around the ocean view and back at his father.

Very confused Maxayus asks. "Father what do you mean?"

Janjii opens his eyes again and stares directly at Maxayus.

Janjii answers Maxayus by saying. "Exactly what I said my boy. I believe the earth is dying losing its life source something beyond these islands is affecting our world, but I cannot process what it is."

Einsberg who is collecting branches near the beach, overheard what Janjii was saying. Einsberg drops the branches and walked a couple of feet towards his hut. Inside the hut Shannon is still sleeping, Einsberg sits on the edge of his straw made bedding. Nervously Einsberg begins to chew on his nails and shake his thigh. This agitation wakes Shannon up, she stares at Einsberg.

Shannon stretches and yawns as she reaches for Henry's shoulder and speaks. "Is everything ok Hun?"

Einsberg holds Shannon's hand that she placed on his shoulder as he responds. "Shannon the earth...... It is dying, the disease out there, I think it has become stronger. I overheard Janjii saying the fish have been dying along with the trees. I also noticed the winds and oceans do not feel like they used to. Who knows what is going on out there!"

Shannon takes a deep breath and speaks. "This is what I was talking about three years ago baby. When I read James's journal, remember?"

Einsberg turns around slowly and looks at Shannon. "We must go back Hun we have to know what is going on out there, our race, humanity, it can all be gone if we waste more time."

Shannon sighs and speaks. “So, we just leave Janjii and his people?? You said they need us here when I asked you, you said we should stay. So, what is it that you really feel baby?

We need to decide on a plan, and we need to decide now!" Einsberg frustrated answers.

“Isn’t the plan to keep the hybrids safe from Theodore?” Shannon replies.

“Yes, I did! But I did not think Theodore would let Humanity die while he holds the cure!!!!"

Shannon with her head down says. “We are no better than Theodore. We could have planned three years ago to go back, instead, we moved to a different island. We could have just gone back Henry!"

Einsberg shouts saying “Even if we do go back now! We still do not have the cure! We cannot take the hybrids unwilling Shannon! We will be no better than those assholes back at that stupid base!"

Shannon stares at Henry with teary eyes and her nostrils flared and speaks. “This is not us Henry! We did not intend for this to happen! I agreed to help the hybrids! But shouting and arguing like this! I am not going to condone this behavior, especially the reason being Theodore!"

Einsberg takes a deep breath while looking at Shannon. Henry hugs Shannon to comfort her.

Shannon cries on his shoulder while Henry rubs her back as he says. “Baby I’m sorry, I didn’t mean to yell or get frustrated with you, I love you."

Shannon wipes her tears and speaks. “I really hate that man.... Henry. Theodore needs to pay for his sins."

Shannon smiles while wiping her tears. She kisses Henry and they both hug.

Henry whispers while hugging Shannon and rubbing her back. “We must think of something and fast. Humanity is counting on us. If Theodore won't tell the world, then we're going to, we have to."

Shannon looks at Henry and she speaks. “Do you think humanity will accept the hybrids even after being cured?"

Henry nods his head and speaks. “I do not know. Humanity may accept them when they need them, but as humans we both know how things go once society begins to forget. The people, the world will have to accept them if they want to live. We will convince them. We must, we are all, the hybrids have into being accepted. We must survive for them. I promised Janjii I will protect them no matter what."

Shannon and Henry hug as both put their foreheads together and close their eyes.

Chapter 6:

A Heartwarming Celebration

Outside a hut we see Spike and Maya walking through the side of the water holding hands. Spike and Maya are both eighteen now and Janjii has told them to meet outside his hut by noon. Spike who has adapted to the island life has longer hair. His hair grew like a palm tree, his hair almost covering his eyes, while the back side hangs under his neck. Spike has also become more agile and stronger. He has learned how to hunt and spar, which he practices with the other males on the island. Maya has also blossomed into a beautiful young woman whose hair reaches her lower back while tied in a French braid.

As Maya and Spike Walk through the side of the islands beach Maya says to Spike. "I wonder what my father wants to talk to us about??"

Spike smiling says. "I'm pretty sure is nothing serious."

Maya stares at Spike smiling, as she stops from walking, she says to Spike. "You have been smiling all week, what is going on???"

Spike also stops walking and holds Mayas hands as he stares into her eyes and says. "Maya ever since the first day I arrived on this island, the moment I saw you, I felt butterflies in my stomach. You have shown and taught me so much in life that I would never have learned on my own. Your brothers and father taught me to fight and defend, all for you."

Maya smiles while caressing Spikes face. "Spike of course we are one now I am also appreciative of you. You have taught me about faith and believing in God, as well as myself, you know I love you."

Spike smiles while holding Maya's hand across his face, kissing her hands gently. "Yes, my love this is why I brought you out here I want to ask you something."

Spike gets on one knee while holding a clam's pearl which is held by a ring that Spike made from some metal.

Spike shows it to Maya and says to her. "Maya, will you Marry me??"

Maya puts her hands over her mouth, eyes watery. "Spike!!! Why yes, I will Spike. I will marry you, my love!"

Maya hugging and kissing Spike then says. "But my father does he know??"

Spike stands up after putting the ring on Maya's hand, he responds. "I asked him before I proposed. He accepted, that's probably what he wants to talk about later."

Maya jumps up like a happy child as she yells out. “Oh yes I'm so excited!"

Maya hugs Spike some more and says to him. “I love You!"

Which Spike replies. “And I you, my Queen."

Back in 656s hut, 656 sits on the edge of the leaves bed.

Luna wakes up as she yawns, she lays her head on 656s back and whispers. “Hey, is it the nightmares again??"

656 smirks. “It’s OK I'll be fine nothing to worry about."

656 holds Lunas hand while he still sits on the edge of bed leaves.

Luna then says to him. “I hear you every night you know, sometimes you twist around so much, you bump me a little. You should talk to the doctors about these nightmares."

656 rolls his eyes as he says. “Why in the hell would I see the doctors about this crap, they are scientists not psychiatrist."

Luna sucks her teeth and nudges 656. She then says. “The same reason you tell me about your dreams; you can tell them you jerk."

656 looks at Luna eye to eye and says to her. “You are my woman is different. Besides, they will not understand."

656 then starts rubbing Luna's belly.

Outside near the beach area of the island we see Rocky who has also grown into a big strong man. Rocky likes to cut his hair with a sharp little knife he got from one of the soldiers. Rocky always stays with short messy hair. Rocky has mastered catching fish he can find, using a Spear. Rocky and Morycus have also built a good relationship since they came to the new island. Because of Rocky's aging he is eighteen now and Morycus is sixteen. While Rocky awaits a fish to pass by, Morycus sits on the beachside rocks watching his friend.

Morycus then says to Rocky. “Do you ever get tired of using the Spear? To me it’s very boring."

Rocky nods his head while still looking into the water ready to launch his spear into the next fish he sees.

Morycus continues to talk as he sits on the Rocks tying a sharp stone to a small wooden pole.

Morycus smiles then says. "I would like to inquire a much different weapon, like the guns we keep stored, when the hybrid soldiers arrived."

Rocky then turns his attention to Morycus and replies. "Hey now, you know those are only for emergency. In case that Sergeant Comes back."

Morycus laughs. "Aaah that got your attention. Besides, it has been three years since, they will not set foot here, we relocated, how will they find us then hmm??"

Rocky turns his attention back towards the water while saying. "Better to be safe than sorry kid, better to be safe."

Rocky throws the spear into the water and catches a fish.

We then move on to the front of Janjiis hut where many hybrids are gathered.

Janjii begins to speak. "Everyone I have gathered you all here today, to make a great announcement. Spike...Maya.... will you two come here please."

Spike and Maya approach Janjii both smiling and holding hands.

"Now My daughter... I have watched you grow into a beautiful woman knowing that a lucky man will win your beauty one day. That man is Spike, and I also knew that one day I would have to let you become your own woman. Well, that day has come my fellow brothers and sisters... for Spike has asked for my blessing, I have accepted, and Maya has accepted Spikes proposal!"

All the hybrids begin to clap and cheer for both Maya and Spike. Mayas Mom Malaya, places a flower necklace around Maya's neck. Then she places one around Spikes' neck. She begins congratulating them both with a kiss on the cheek. Reedriake just walks away as everyone cheers, Reedriake with a very disturbed look in his face.

Later, that night everyone celebrates Spike and Mayas engagement. Everyone is having a fun time laughing and dancing. The tribe is playing drums out of coconuts and a recorder made of sticks. Rocky is being silly with the kids, 656 is cuddled by the fire with Luna, while Shannon and Einsberg dance together along with Codwell and Standford. Spike and Maya are doing a walk-through seashell as part of a tradition the hybrids produced. Everyone seems happy. Meanwhile, Maxayus and Morycus converse with their father by the bonfire.

Chapter 7:

Where there's Hope......

Janjii sits in front of the bonfire on his right Maxayus the oldest son and on Janjiis left Morycus the youngest son. The three have gathered to discuss the situation with the food source on the island.

Janjii starts by saying. "Now Boys remember what I said, do not inform anyone today what we have noticed, we do not want to worry everyone. Today is the celebration for Spike and your sister Maya."

Maxayus and Morycus both look at each other and agree.

Maxayus then speaks. "Father I was on the north side of the island today. Dozens of fish washed up shore all dead."

Morycus also adds on to his day. "This afternoon seagulls were found in the small woods, Father none were attacked or had wounds."

Janjii stares into the bonfire while saying. "This is something much more then, my sons we must stay aware."

Maxayus watching his father stare into the bonfire takes a deep breath and asks. "Father did you not experience anything like this back at the base??"

Janjii looks at Maxayus as he nods. "No son this is different."

Janjii continues talking to the boys, but they hear a loud scream coming from the celebration. Everyone stops what they are doing and head towards where the dancing was happening. There they see Ryan Stanford face planted on the sand twitching. Einsberg immediately rushes to him and turns him over, he seems pale and is foaming out the mouth. Einsberg quickly tries to sit Ryan up while everyone gathers and watches. Einsberg tries to pick Ryan up, to take him into a new medical hut built on the new island.

Einsberg says to everyone. "Stand back! Please!"

Stacy cries and shouts. "Henry, is he going to be, ok??"

Einsberg avoiding the question continues to try and get help for his friend.

He asks some hybrids for help. "Let's take him in the hut now!"

Two other warriors help Einsberg carry Ryan back into the hut, as everyone else watches in disbelief. Spike runs in behind them. They all enter the hut and set Ryan down on a bed of Dead Palm leaves.

Spike rushes next to Henry asking. "What happened?"

Einsberg is opening Ryan's eyelids and checking his pulse while he answers Spike. "I do not know he is still breathing.... Maybe he's having a seizure."

Shannon walks in between Spike and Henry holding James's book and speaks. "No, it's not a seizure."

Einsberg turns towards Shannon and asks. "Is it what I think?"

Shannon holds James's book and hands it to Henry. "It is all in there, the symptoms, how it starts. James described it when his wife and child went through the same thing."

Spike takes a deep breath and asks. "Can't we just use our blood to help him??"

Einsberg pauses and looks towards Spike, while handing the book back to Shannon and speaks. "It is not that Simple Spike. First, we need a machine that will take out the blood, a syringe to inject it and other fluids as well. We have none of that with us we."

Einsberg pauses and then hysterically screams out. "We must leave! We must leave now!!!"

Einsberg starts to cry as he lays his head on his friend's unconscious body. Shannon falls to her knees while holding James's book, Spike looks around the room as everyone seems silent. Spike stares at everyone as if time is moving slowly.

Spike closes his eyes and says in his head. "Lord, I am thankful for your protection and your strength. I am weak...but that is ok because YOU are strong for me. I praise you for that!"

Spike opens his eyes again and asks Henry. "Henry how do you plan to go back we need to calm down and think about how we all can help. Ryan is our friend as well; we all can help."

Henry stops weeping for a second and pulls himself together. Henry looks at Spike and speaks. "The boat Spike, the boat can take us far. It has gas in its storage; we can make it to the city."

Spike nods his head. Then Spike speaks. "As soon as you get to the city Theodore will know, he will come after you and succeed."

Henry then responds to Spike. "Ryan is dying this is more important than Theodore right now!"

Spike looks at Henry face to face and speaks. "What is important is that we all stay alive, and we all stick together. I am not losing my family again! You, Shannon, and everyone! You will not die under my watch or put yourselves in danger!"

Henry sighs and responds. "Spike!!! We have no choice!! Humanity is dying out there we need to go!!"

Spike looks at Henry in disappointment. Spike under his breath says. "There has to be a better way, there's just got to be."

Spike then walks out of the hut. Spike heads towards his hut and sits on his bed of leaves inside. He bows his head while folding his palms.

Maya enters the hut and sits next to Spike, she asks. "What are you thinking about my love?"

Spike picks his head up while putting his hand on Mayas. "I do not know what to do my love. I feel as though I am failing the Doctors. They say it is not as simple as drawing blood from us. They need equipment and medical supplies that we do not have."

Maya takes a deep breath and speaks. "So, they must leave then? Correct?"

Spike nods his head and puts it down again as he still sits in his bed. "I do not want them to get hurt out there. Theodore will find them and harm them. I feel helpless, I feel as though I have to let them go, but a part of me does not want to allow them to leave."

Maya rubs Spike shoulders and speaks. "You must go with them my love."

Spike picks his head up and looks at Maya. "What? No, my love, I will not leave you!"

Maya smiles and speaks. "You will return my king; it is just to protect the doctors. I have faith you will return. I will pray for all of you to come back safely."

Spike smiles and speaks. "My love, I cannot.... My place is here with you."

Maya puts both her hands on Spikes cheeks and says to him. "My king, as your future wife, your future carrier of your children. I cannot watch you worry about what is in your heart. In your heart is passion and love for everyone, this being the reason I fell in love with you. I know you want to help; do not worry about me, I will be here. But you, you need to do what you are passionate about and that is to help those you love."

Spike smiles and puts his forehead gently on Maya's forehead. "Oh, how you know me so well my queen."

Maya smiles and speaks. "Do what's right my king I will always support you."

Spike picks his head up feeling like a new person full of energy, he kisses Maya and stands up as he says. "I will go and tell the Doctors in the morning that I will be traveling with them."

Maya smiles and stands up with Spike and speaks. "I will be here when you return my love, may God be with you on your journey and may he protect you from the evil of the world."

Chapter 8:

Rerouting……

That same night after the commotion has calmed down, everyone returns to their huts. The team of scientists have decided to take Ryan Standford back to the closest city. According to Henry, Straton City seems to be the closest. Straton City is four hours away on boat from the island, it is also the best place to get resources, before Theodore finds them. Only problem is what they believe is not true, especially after what happened with Team AdreNaline back in James's warehouse, which is in Straton City. Henry has already spoken to Janjii about leaving in the morning, which Janjii sadly agreed.

That evening in 656s hut, he begins to toss and turn very heavily, causing Luna who sleeps next to him to awaken. Luna watches 656 as he begins to toss and turn, then he stops as he stops, he pauses for a good five seconds and out of nowhere he begins to twitch and shake.

Lunas eyes grow wide as she screams for help. "Someone!! Please help!!!" Luna shouts.

656 starts to shake as if he is having a seizure. Luna keeps shouting, then 656 stops and wakes up sitting up fast and breathing heavy. He turns to see Luna out of her bed crying and yelling for help.

656 walks over to her calmly saying. "Hey, hey what's wrong?"

Luna grabs 656 face while still crying and says very quietly. "You need to get help...... you were shaking and choking...... I yelled for help, and no one came...... I need you please to get help."

Luna breaks down crying and 656 tries to keep her calm by comforting her and hugging her. 656 says nothing while calming Luna down as both are on the floor comforting one another.

After a while 656 says to Luna. "It's going to be ok; it's going to be okay."

Luna falls back to sleep cuddled in 656s arm, while 656 just stares around thinking to himself. "I was drowning again in my dream; I have to find out what the hell is going on before I die in my sleep."

The next morning Luna walks into the hut as the Scientists are preparing to leave. Henry and Shannon both look at Luna in a concerned manner.

Luna politely says, "Excuse me Doctors??"

Shannon walks towards Luna and asks her. "Yes, Luna how may we help? Is the baby alright??"

Luna chuckles as she rubs her own belly and replies. "Yes, the baby's all right, thank you for asking Ms. Shannon but.... Well, it's... it's about 656." Luna whispers.

Henry approaches Luna with concern and asks. "What is it, Luna? What is wrong with 656?"

Luna then tells Einsberg about 656 nightmares. Luna says. "See he has been having these weird nightmares every night, they are getting worse. It has gotten to the point where he keeps me up at night. Like last night, he looked like he was...... like he was having a seizure doctors, it does not seem normal to me anymore. I felt like he was drowning in real life, and I couldn't do anything to help."

Einsberg then asks Luna. "Has he ever mentioned what is happening in his dreams? Anything he has shared with you about the nightmares?"

Luna then begins to explain to Henry about the nightmares 656 has shared with her. "Well, he says he finds himself in a capsule full of water with things connected on his body. He also mentions before entering seeing the numbers... "Gate 2-B."

Einsbergs eyes widened as he looks at Luna and speaks. "Wait....wait!! Gate 2-B?? What else has he mentioned?"

Luna then pauses and begins to worry, she looks around and says. "Is there something I should be worried about doctor? Is there something you know?"

Einsberg calmly tells Luna. "It's just a little more information I need from his nightmares, do you know where I can find him right now Luna?"

Luna replies. "Yes, he went for a walk.... He's by the beach area."

Einsberg replies. "Thank you, Luna."

Einsberg quickly walks out of the hut and looks for 656 as he finds him just staring into the water. Einsberg slowly walks over to 656 from his right side and says to him. "Good morning."

656 looks at Einsberg then looks away, while saying. "What is it Einsberg?"

Einsberg sits next to 656 and speaks. “Hey Luna told me about the nightmares you’re having??"

656 smiles. “That woman worries too much."

Einsberg giggles and replies. “Well, she cares about you 656, she wants the best for you especially when you two are starting a family."

656 smiles again as he plays with the sand between his fingers. He asks Henry. “So, what is it that she told you?"

Einsberg takes a deep breath and asks. “Is it true that every time you dream you see the number-"

Right before Henry can finish his sentence, 656 finishes it for him as he blurts out. "Gate 2-B. For as long as I can remember that’s a number I can't forget."

Einsberg staring at 656 with an unbelievable look says to him. “Listen that number and word it says. "Gate" I have been in that place before. It was a military airbase I believe it’s been shut down a long time ago just left deserted, all the equipment, all supplies just left behind...."

As Einsberg pauses for a second, he realizes that he may have just found the answer to help Ryan and humanity while looking at 656.

656 asks Einsberg. “Do you mean this place is real???"

Einsberg says nothing and begins to think.

656 then shouts. “Einsberg say something you fool!!"

Einsberg puts his hand on 656s shoulder and 656 quickly looks at Einsbergs hand.

Einsberg then says. “Listen to me I have a plan. We can go to this base, ok? You may find your answers and why these dreams happen."

656 raises his eyebrow and speaks. "Are you mad??? You will go with me just because of a dream???"

Einsberg replies. "Listen to me last I heard the facility was shut down and all supplies were left behind. This is perfect, this is exactly what we need...... We can save Ryan and humanity. We can also find out why your dreams show this place, which you have never even heard. It's not that far either, a map I need to find the map, it should be on James's boat he arrived on."

Einsberg then remembers. "Ah wait there's one here I have it, I forgot I took it to travel to Straton City later on."

656 looks at Henry and speaks. "Have you gone mad Einsberg, calm yourself. First, how far is this place?"

Einsberg looks at the map and starts to calculate from the island to the base. He does this by seeing the time it takes from the island to Straton City which is four hours away. Since the island is not on the map he goes by that.

Then he finds the location of the base and speaks. "About two hours so it will be four hours up and back we can do it. We can also get fuel there."

656 nods his head as he says to Einsberg. "What if this base isn't shut down anymore?"

Einsberg then replies. "It is shut down because the military lost money and there is no way they gained any of it back after the war. Especially now with this disease becoming more deadly."

656 says. "Damn it you better be right......OK I will go but.... I need another favor."

Einsberg then asks. "What? What is it?"

656 stands up and speaks. Get me out of this damn tribe gear and give me the gear we stored from the base and some damn guns. I am not going somewhere unknown without my weapons."

Einsberg laughs as he pats 656 on his back and speaks. "Ok deal!"

The weapons are kept on the boat where they are guarded by Rocky, along with the clothes of the Hybrids that arrived from the base. Einsberg informs Janjii of what is happening. Janjii agrees to let him go on this expedition as he too believes in Einsberg finding help. Spike who is walking towards Einsberg and Janjii at this moment overhears half the conversation.

Spike then says. "Hey!!! I am coming with you."

656 nods his head and says to Spike. "Stay here kid this doesn't concern you!"

Spike looks at 656 and speaks. "Listen 656 I owe you a lot, you brought me to this island and if it wasn't for you, I would have never met Maya and learn the things I know."

656 then replies. "Which is exactly why you should stay. You are about to get married should you not stay here with your future wife?"

Spike replies. "Listen to me I'm going, you need me anyway, I can be helpful, there is a lot I learned from my father's book, I know it better than anyone and weather you want to hear it or not, you, yourself are leaving behind a pregnant woman."

656 smiles and speaks. "I like you kid always have."

Einsberg then says to 656. "He is right 656, we need all the help we can get.

As they approach the boat with all the gear, they see Rocky who is guarding the boat. Rocky must make sure no one goes and tries to take the weapons.

Rocky sees everyone approaching and uncrosses his arms and speaks. "Hey Spike, Einsberg.... number guy. What can I help you with??"

Spike says to Rocky. “We need the boat, Rocky; we got a little emergency here."

Rocky looks confused and speaks. “What kind of emergency?”

Spike then tells Rocky. “It’s a long story."

Spike hops on the boat and begins untying the rope of the boat. Rocky looks around and sees everyone hoping on the boat.

Rocky then asks Spike. “Wait a minute Spike what about Maya?!"

656 laughs and speaks. “I said the same thing!"

Spike nods his head and says to everyone. “Thanks for the concern but trust me when I say this. Maya has no problem with me going."

Rocky shrugs his shoulders and speaks. “Well guess I'm going too."

656 quickly turns to Rocky and shouts. “Oh, hell no that’s enough people already!"

Rocky responds. “Screw you man that’s my bro; I'm going no matter what."

As Spike and 656 untie the boat, they start putting on the soldiers' gear and clothes. Shannon comes over and hops onto the boat.

Einsberg rushes towards her and speaks. “Shannon what are you doing??"

Shannon starts to grab some clothes and says to Henry. “I'm going!"

Einsberg shakes his head and speaks. “No!! You need to stay here with Ryan and Stacey!!"

Shannon turns to Henry and speaks. "Janjii told us about this expedition when I asked, how is it that Maya and Luna know their men are going but not me."

Spike and 656 look at Einsberg as if he is in trouble.

Einsberg smiling says. "Really??? You are upset because I did not inform you??"

Shannon replies while tying her hair up in a bun. "Stacey told me to go; she wants to be alone with Ryan. Oh, and Spike you almost forgot this."

Stacey Hands Spike James's book.

Spike says. "Thank you."

Einsberg then starts the boat smiling as everyone gets comfortable.

Rocky asks. "So, where the hell are we going exactly?"

Einsberg begins to pick up some speed as he heads west from the island and replies to Rocky. "To save lives my friend, to save lives."

656 and the boys start to raise the sail as the boat starts moving away from the island, some of the tribe members wave goodbye and the boat slowly starts to drift away from the tribe's view.

Chapter 9:

A Flashback.......

This flashback takes place after Sergeant Luther tried to take over the hybrids island. Not only did he fail, but the soldier hybrids turned against him and made him flee off the island. In the mist of the hybrid's rebellion, Spike at that time, fifteen years old, used a knife and stabbed the Sergeant in his right eye. The Sergeant fled with all the other Sergeants on board, took off back to Theodore's restricted island and this is where we pick up in this flashback. The Sergeant arrives at Theodore's island storming through the halls. He has so much anger that he is not concerned or notices he is leaving a trail of blood coming from his eye socket all over Theodore's marble floor. Sergeant Luther is heading straight to Theodore's office where we see Theodore on his phone, sitting looking out his window at the ocean view.

We can hear Theodore's conversation. "Yes now I have told you we have plans, did I not? Yes I understand your people are dying my people are also dying..... now listen-"

Theodore then gets interrupted by the door slamming wide open caused by Sergeant Luther himself. Sergeant Luther looks at Theodore with a raging anger; Luther holds both doors open while breathing heavily looking like one of the undead. Blood dripping down his right eye socket like if he has been crying bloody tears. His hair messy as if he just got electrocuted by a strike of lightning. Theodore turns to see who has slammed open his door, there he sees the Sergeant who looks like a mess.

Theodore then continues his conversation on the phone by saying. "General let me call you back....... Yes...... Yes I will Buh bye."

Theodore then hangs up the phone. He looks at Luther with his hands crossed as he awaits for Luther's explanation, but instead Luther begins to throw a fit.

The Sergeant starts to scream. "I will kill them all I swear!!! You tell me right now, right now Theodore and I will do it! I will send a whole nuclear missile to that god damn island!!! Just let me do it! let me be the one to do it!!! I want to put a camera as well, so I can watch all of them melt and burn as they suffer!!"

Theodore just pours himself a glass of vodka while Luther is lashing out all his frustration. Theodore takes a sip; he watches Luther continue to yell.

"Those god damn hybrids turned on me, they united!!! Oh, and that...... That damn ...... James's hybrid I will kill them all!!!"

Theodore then speaks after he swallows his drink. "Ah yes about James.... you did kill him did you not?"

Luther looks at Theodore with a shocking look.

Theodore then says. "Now let's have a look at your eye, let me see what they did."

Luther leans in and shows Theodore his whole eye socket with no eye in it. Theodore observes the eye as if he is astonished by the sight.

Theodore then says. "My, my they really got you good didn't they??"

The Sergeant backs away and calmly but angrily says. "Listen to me, I know the location give me soldiers we can trust and I'll go back, I can-"

Theodore interrupts the Sergeant by saying. "Now, now relax you know I cannot do that! Did you get James? You never answered my question."

Luther takes a deep breath then yells. "I shot half of his fucking Brains out I got him!!!"

Which Theodore responds with. "Good at least you lost your eye for a reason now didn't you?"

The Sergeant bangs his hands on Theodore's desk as he shouts. "I want them all dead, every single one!!!"

Theodore stands up from his chair and faces the Sergeant.

Theodore with his hands on his desk then says to Luther. "Calm yourself Sergeant That is an order. We cannot go back with our own soldiers I would have to fill reports etc., etc. People will ask why our troops are on this island, soldiers will go back and say what they saw, then everything will be a big mess understand?"

Sergeant Luther with a confused look says. "But.... What.... About.... The god damn Scientists!!"

Theodore sits back down and responds. "Listen to me my good friend we will have our moment, but not now the disease has spread worldwide half of Africa and Central America has been wiped. I just got off the phone with General Ratnier he said Russia is losing population also they are trying to cut a deal with us involving the four tunnels."

Luther then sits down in the chair across Theodore's desk. "I thought we had an agreement on the four tunnels already?!"

Theodore replies. "Yes but they are willing to give us more rights to the tunnels if we can find a cure. The plan is going accordingly; we knew the Russians will panic in a pandemic and start looking towards us for help."

Luther asks confusingly. "Sir we already have the cure what are you talking about??"

Theodore smiles. "Yes we do but the Russians don't know that and neither does the rest of the world."

The Sergeant grabs a glass cup and begins to pour himself a glass of Theodore's vodka. "So, what are you planning then?" Sergeant Luther asks.

Theodore takes the bottle and pours himself another glass. "Well, I already have a team to replace James's old team. Remember we need a team that the public thinks is looking for some kind of cure to keep the people calm. But do you remember that book we found in Ms. Delbrys house?"

Luther nods his head.

Theodore continues to speak. "Well, she made valid points. See there is a section where she asks.

"What if the hybrids blood is injected in other animals?"

This made me think so I sent this info to our 2nd group of Scientist who create the hybrids back at the old base." The Sergeant clears his throat and confusingly asks. "Didn't you shut that base down?"

Theodore begins to laugh. "Oh, Sergeant I apologize but there are secrets even you do not know. But back to the conversation, I had to make people think it was shut down to get investigators off my back. But there are still scientists there."

Luther smiles and asks. "So, what did they discover??" Theodore slams his cup on the desk. "They have discovered that with the blood of the hybrids you CAN create other hybrid species!!! Amazing isn't it?! How one question can be answered through curiosity!!"

Theodore then starts to laugh maniacally. Luther with a look of confusion says. "So, what are you saying? We are going to start building a fucking zoo??"

Theodore nods his head. "No, no, no my dear friend this is only a test to see how far the blood goes, whatever animals transform get put down of course. We do not want another incident like the one you went through and the situation with your experiment soldier who escaped. But we are getting closer to having full global control back to this country."

Luther then asks. "So how sure are you that the Russians will agree on more rights to the tunnels? Just because they are losing control, it does not mean they are going to give us more access to the tunnels. Hell, the whole reason we built the tunnels is because they wanted us to show them loyalty after losing the war. Are you just going to keep letting the world die out until they do give us the rights?"

Theodore looks at Luther seriously and says. "That is the plan for now my dear friend as you can see I am terribly busy. As long as they believe we are working on this cure they will give us what we ask."

Luther then asks Theodore. "When will you make it publicly?"

Theodore just smiles and says. "Oh, and by the way I wanted to know more on this 656 experiment, the second group sent me his info when he was created, I think you would want to read this."

Theodore Hands Luther 656s portfolio. Luther's eyes grow wide. "Is this possible!?"

Theodore smiles and says. "Well, he is walking around alive isn't he?"

Luther reads the file some more and says. "Oh, this makes me want to kill that son of a bitch even more now."

Theodore laughs. "You'll get your chance my dear friend, you will but be patient once we have the rights to the tunnels we will have more equipment, more supplies and a better chance to find what I'm looking for, just be patient."

Theodore then gets an idea. "Sergeant as a matter of fact, maybe there is a way you can take your frustration out on that experiment 656."

Luther replies. "I'm listening." Theodore begins to explain. "I had some insight on an FBI team; they are special Opps or something. Get this, they discovered something in James' abandoned warehouse in Straton City, now just to be safe, I had inside sources investigate the area first. Problem is that since the FBI are cracking down on these government affairs, that special Opps team has already been called to also investigate."

Luther then asks. "So, what is it that you're asking of me?"

Theodore hands the Sergeant the files to Team AdreNaline. Luther begins to read them, then Luther starts to laugh.

Luther grabs Theodore face and says. "You bastard!! You should have shown me this when I was pissed a couple of minutes ago!"

Luther laughs hysterically.

Theodore smiles and says. "That is why I kept asking you about James even after his death that son of a bitch is still fucking up my plans. Well, I have some special operations personal ready to go as well. I figured you'd want the mission after everything I informed you with."

Luther laughs and loudly says. "You're damn right!!"

Theodore laughs. "Alright go on then get cleaned up and head out. Do not worry about making a little bit of noise. I have had my insiders block off half the area just in case you need to get messy. Oh, and Luther, remember if our side happens to get injured..... No survivors."

Luther laughs and takes the files with him as he walks out of Theodore's room, like a child who just got permission to do whatever he wants. Theodore sits alone in his chair and picks up the phone, only to get back to his conversation he had earlier before Luther stormed right in.

Chapter 10:

A Journey to Remember

While out on sea everyone on the boat seems quiet. The boat ride has felt like everyone has been sailing for days now. Rocky is sitting next to Spike while Spike reads James's book. 656 stares at the ocean while standing up near the sail and Shannon stands next Einsberg while he drives the boat.

Rocky then breaks the silence by loudly shouting. "Holy crap! How much longer do we have? It feels like it has been a week at sea!!!"

Einsberg looks at an old timer the boat has displayed and says. "Well even though this boat doesn't read the right time, I'm going by how much time has passed, we should be getting closer; I say maybe another thirty minutes."

Rocky then shouts again. "Thirty more minutes!!! What the hell man damn it!! I should have just stayed; I would be spearing some fish right now!!!

656 then replies. "Yea I wish you'd had stayed back in the island as well."

Spike then closes James book and asks. "So, this base? What is it actually?"

Einsberg replies while still driving the boat. "Well Spike, it actually was an old military airbase, but after the war the army couldn't continue to operate this base due to the expenses the country suffered."

Shannon then says to Einsberg. "Henry did you not hear what supposedly was being said about this base?"

Einsberg turns to Shannon with a confused look and says. "What do you mean? Last I heard it was abandoned."

Shannon looks around at everyone and then says to Einsberg. "Hun I thought you knew.. the base was rumored to be where all hybrids were created."

Einsberg quickly says. "What?! When was this rumored??"

Shannon replies. "As soon as I took the oath to care for the hybrids back at the training base. I thought this is why you thought to come here for supplies?"

656 quickly approaches Einsberg and says. "You see I knew this place wasn't going to be abandoned, what the hell do we do now Einsberg?!"

Einsberg with a look of concern says out loud. "Hey, let us calm down ok? We will be simply fine. Just let me think!"

Einsberg continues driving and looks at 656. Einsberg notices 656 is wearing military gear from when the military hybrids came on the island. Einsberg then looks ahead and begins to see the silhouette of the base up ahead.

Einsberg quickly shouts while looking at the base. “Ok listen everyone we’re all going to have to wear some of the military uniforms on board just in case we see military personnel there."

656 says. “Oh yea and then what Einsberg? We tell them we got lost with a boat out on sea??"

Einsberg then replies. “No me and Shannon will function as military personnel and the rest of you will function as hybrid experiments accompanying us."

656 shakes his head and begins to load his pistol with bullets. 656 then notices Rocky and Spike staring at him.

656 tells the boys. “Listen you guys watched action movies right?"

The boys look at each other and nod yes. 656 then continues. “Ok look this is how you load a gun, after you load the clip you place it back in the gun. You then cock it back here on the top of the gun, aim and then pull the trigger understand?"

Rocky says. “Hell yeah!"

Rocky takes the pistol and gladly puts it on his hip side. 656 then hands one to Spike, but Spike stares at the other pistol and shakes his head.

656 raises his eyebrow and says. “Kid take the gun! We do not know what we are dealing with once we reach that base!"

Spike then responds. “That is a dangerous weapon if I am going to defend myself I will just fight. There is no reason why I did all that training back on the island, if I am not going to use the techniques that were taught to me."

656 smirks and says. “Kid I’m pretty sure you are a hell of a fighter, but if these people on here have guns you can’t just fight back with fists, its suicide kid."

Spike replies. “I’ll take my chances with faith."

656 nods his head and says. “Sometimes kid not even God can protect you from what this world hits you with, sometimes you got to put faith aside and put survivability ahead."

Spike without looking at 656 just says. “Survivability is considered having faith, you are acting as a defense mechanism which is your survival instinct, but while instinct has giving you the strength and faith to make you believe, you will survive and you are ready for what’s to come. My survival instinct is faith itself, so with faith I am confident enough that my fighting skills will protect me along with the power of God."

656 smiles and Rocky says. “Damn bro you are a badass with your words. Look, you left number guy shut, look at him he has nothing to say."

656 continues to smile at Spike and then replies to Spike while putting away the pistol he was trying to give Spike.

“Hey kid?"

Spike turns to 656 and then 656 says to Spike while still smiling. “You mind saying a little prayer for us?"

Spike smiles and puts his hand on 656 shoulder as he says. "Thank You for increasing my faith as I step forward into the unknown. Thank You for teaching me to trust. And thank You that even though I cannot see what immediately is ahead, I know the end. I know that because of Christ, my ultimate future is with You in eternity amen."

Everyone on the boat had their head down and repeated “Amen". Einsberg who kept his eyes straight ahead, chin up was letting the prayer sink in his body. 656 nods his head to Spike and continues to look forward towards the islands silhouette.

Rocky begins to grab the military uniforms from the boats storage and starts to pass the uniforms around to everyone that is not wearing one. Shannon goes to the back of the boat to change while Rocky is changing inside the captain's deck. Spike also begins to change out of his tribal gear and into the uniforms. Einsberg starts to put on the shirt while driving and quickly gearing his trousers, while maintaining a hand on the wheel of the boat. Everyone is suited up and looking like army personnel. We then see the boat getting closer to the base where the waves become a little heavier and noisy than before. The scene then pans upwards towards the base, which looks like a creepy rock island with a dock on the side and a long set of stairs leading to the top of the Rocky Mountain. The Rocky Island itself gives off an eerie feeling just by the looks of it. It is abandoned like Einsberg thought it was, but what is on the inside? What awaits everyone who approaches this odd-looking base? 656 looks at the base and takes a deep breath, his anxiety gets more intense as the boat approaches closer to the base.

Chapter 11:

Tensions........

Back at the Island, we can see Janjii cooking out of a big metal pot. The pot amazingly was made by none other than Spike. Spike used some of the metals from extra guns that were not needed, due to them having too much corrosion from not being used. Janjii seems to be breaking some sort of pine leaves into the pot. He is making a sort of soup, which looks like a homemade remedy of some sort. Janjii pours some onto a big leaf bowl, held on by some bamboo shaped like a saucer. Janjii then walks with the bowl towards a hut, there in the hut, we can see Stacey caressing Ryan while he is lying on his leaf bed. Janjii approaches the two with the bowl in his hand. Ryan is too weak to sit up but smiles while staring at Janjii.

Ryan says very weakly. "Thank you Janjii."

Stacey grabs the bowl and puts it slowly in Ryan's lips, she tilts the bowl a little and Ryan slowly sips the soup.

Janjii is crouched down in front of Ryan and Janjii says to him. “I made from the pines on the island, mixed a little with some shrimp I found, it’s fresh out the fire my friend, it'll give you some energy."

Ryan sips the soup and says to Janjii still with a weak tone. “Thank you Janjii, I really appreciate you my friend, you are very kind."

Janjii puts his hand on Ryan’s head and says to him. “Save your energy, Sir Ryan..... rest now friend.... rest."

Stacey looks at Janjii and whispers to him in a sad tone. “Thank you Janjii."

Janjii wipes the tears off Stacey’s eyes and responds to her by saying. “It is the best I can do for my family; I will let you both rest now. Please feel free to come and find me Ms. Stacey if I am needed."

Stacey smiles and gives Janjii a nod of appreciation. Janjii then walks out of the hut and looks around while taking a deep breath. Janjii begins to observe everyone on the island and then he notices Reedriake. Reedriake is sitting on a tree towards the small woods of the island. Janjii walks over to the tree, Janjii looks up to see Reedriake just staring out into the open.

Janjii then says to Reedriake. “My boy what are doing up there?"

Reedriake rolls his eyes but still replies to Janjii. “Just enjoying the view from up here Janjii!"

Janjii then says to Reedriake. “Come down my boy I want a word with you."

Reedriake looks annoyed but out of respect for Janjii he jumps down from the tree. Reedriake stares at Janjii awaiting his word.

Janjii puts his hand on Reedriakes left shoulder and says to him. “Reedriake, you have not been the same since you lost your friend from that day. Is it still bothering you dear boy?"

Reedriakes lets out a chuckle and rubs his chin while still smiling.

Reedriake then looks at Janjii and says. "You know what bothers me Janjii, is the fact that the man who killed my friend, had a proper funeral."

Janjii becomes a little more concerned but still calmly tells Reedriake. "Yes, my boy but we must respect all those who pass, remembering only their life, not the bad things they did."

Reedriake facial expression changes from a smirk to a more subtle. Reedriake looks away as if he is done with the conversation but then turns his attention back to Janjii.

Reedriake then says. "You know Janjii, if it weren't for that visitor Maya will Marry, those things that occurred would have never came to be. The man who killed my friend, the others that were attacked, oh and let's not forget now, we've had to relocate islands."

Janjii takes a deep breath and responds to Reedriake. "Yes, my friend, but things happen for a reason, sometimes our path becomes difficult, but our journey will lead us to the direction God has written for us, always remember that my boy."

Reedriake stares at Janjii with his chin up and his chest out.

Reedriake smirks again and asks. "Janjii, do you recall before that visitor came, that you wanted me to take Maya's hand in marriage?"

Janjii becomes a little annoyed with this question but proceeds to answer Reedriake. "Yes, I do recall Reedriake, why do you ask this question?"

Reedriake then says. "Ah, just wondering if that was something that was already written, as I recall... you also mentioned to me that I would be the best chief this island has to offer, has that changed my path as well?"

Janjii now becomes more serious as he to pokes his chest out and raises his chin.

Reedriake then says to Janjii. “So, you told me lies to make me feel proud? Is that your plan? Or is it that you just felt sorry for me, because of what happened to my father?"

Before Reedriake begins to breakdown, Janjii interrupts Reedriake and says. “Reedriake, I did not tell you lies, I do not control Mayas heart my daughter makes her own choices. As for the promise to be Chief, my boy I was stating an opinion and my opinion remains the same. But my lineage lies with Maxayus, Maya and Morycus so whomever they choose to be with, will become part of my lineage my boy."

Reedriake turns away with anger, but Janjii still speaks as he says. “The accident with your father is not the reason I tell you this. What happened to your father was not your fault, this also drew me closer to you, I feel as though you are one of my sons Reedriake."

Reedriake then interrupts Janjii and angrily says. “Yes, but you must guide your daughter the right way!!! That outsider is no good for Maya, and you know it!!"

Janjii becomes frustrated and finally tells Reedriake. “Listen to me, we will not discuss my daughter’s life, you understand me!! You do not speak of Maya's love life or question it with me understood??!!”

Reedriake calms down takes a deep breath and says to Janjii. “I understand Janjii, please forgive me."

Reedriake puts his right hand on his own chest and slightly bows to Janjii.

Janjii looks at Reedriake and responds. “You are forgiven my boy; I will leave you in peace now."

As Janjii turns around and walks back towards the village, Reedriake holds his hatchet with rage. He then looks at Janjii as if he wants to hit him, like he did to his own friend three years ago. As soon Reedriake takes a step behind Janjii, Maxayus appears right behind Reedriake. Maxayus says. "Everything alright Reedriake??"

Reedriake smiles and slightly turns his head towards Maxayus as he responds with.

"Everything is fine good friend; everything is just fine."

As Reedriake walks away, Maxayus gives him a very odd stare. Just then Morycus can be seen running behind Maxayus and yelling out at his brother.

Morycus says. "Maxayus!! Quickly come brother!"

Maxayus then begins to follow his brother. Morycus runs straight to the beach area on the other side of the island, as they approach the beach side Maxayus's eyes grow wide. Maxayus then sees whales, sharks and other sea animals washed up on the shore all dead.

Morycus then asks Maxayus. "Is this what Father was mentioning the other night Maxayus?"

Maxayus says nothing while still looking at the horrific scene.

Maxayus then snaps out of his head and tells Morycus. "Go fetch father Morycus....... Quickly!"

Morycus responds. "Yes brother, right away!"

Morycus runs towards the village where he finds Janjii.

Morycus tells Janjii. "Father... you are needed on the other side of the beach, hurry!"

Janjii signals other nearby warriors to come with him. Meanwhile back at the beachside. Maxayus stares into the graveyard of sea mammals washed up. Maxayus is in utter shock of what he is looking upon. All these Creatures dead. As Janjii approaches the beachside with Morycus along with the other hybrid warriors, everyone just pauses for a while. The sunsets and the orange sky starts to turn dark; no one says a word as they all watch in horror. Janjii mutters. "God, protect and help us all."

Chapter 12:

Abandoned.........

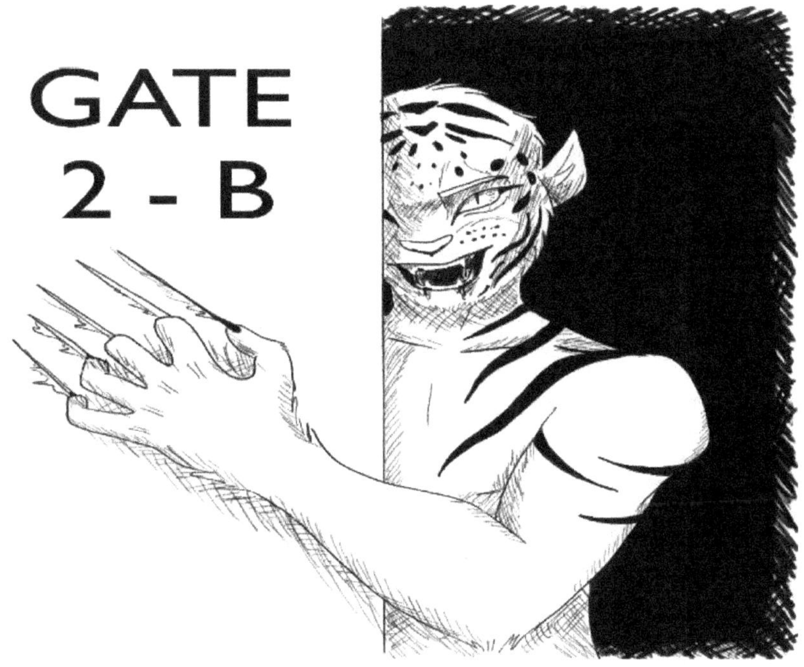

Einsberg begins to set the boat on the side approaching a wooden dock, which is found on the left side of the Rocky Island base. The base has three entrances to arrive on. There is a cave way for the boats, which is where Einsberg must dock. Then up on top of the mountain, there is a helicopter Landing and a strip for aircrafts to land on. The group is emerging through the cave, which is a path that leads to a clifflike structure with a stairway leading to what looks like the top of the base. Einsberg approaches the dock and begins mooring. The group begins to disembark from the boat. Spike is looking up at the cave like structure, meanwhile 656 is equipping himself with more weapons. 656 carries a rifle on his back along with his pistol located on his hip. Einsberg also puts a pistol on his back area where his pants hold the gun. Rocky puts his gun on his hip and

Shannon carries a rifle on her back. Rocky looks around as if he is the last one to disembark.

Rocky then says. "So, this is it huh?"

Einsberg looks around and replies. "Yes, it looks different from the last time I was here."

Einsberg then says to everyone. "Right over here everyone! We just have to walk up these stairs and pass a gate."

Everyone follows Einsberg with 656 right after Henry. As the group approaches the chain link gate a sign on it reads. "NO TRESPASSING." Just above that sign 656 sees another sign that reads. "Gate 2-A."

Einsberg looks at 656 and jokingly says. "Well, I guess Gate 2-B is around here huh?"

656 nods his head and the group continue to slowly enter the gate. As the group enter the gate, they are now located on the mountain top of the base. There the group sees aircraft, helicopters, and some abandoned jets. The place looks like an abandoned airport yard. The setting is very gloomy and foggy. Shannon looks around and notices ripped army clothes across the yard.

She then whispers to Einsberg. "Eins, are you seeing this??"

Einsberg looks around and his eyes grow wide.

Shannon then says. "Henry its soldiers!! All ripped to pieces, look there has been some sort of fighting going on here!!"

656 then adds by saying. "Einsberg the bullet shells don't look that old, wasn't this supposedly just a creation base?"

Einsberg confusingly replies. "That is what the rumor was. This does not seem right at all. Come let's go find the entrance to the facility, it looks like it's only a couple of feet ahead."

The group continues to walk cautiously towards the second chain link gate. Behind that gate is a building that looks like a facility. As the group walks closer to the Entrance they hear a loud roar, echoing through the walkway of the gate. Rocky begins to sniff and starts to growl.

Rocky then crouches in a fighting defensive stance and says. "I don't like what that smells like you guys!!"

The group except Spike, all draw their weapons towards the sound of the roar. Spike stares around the whole area. Spike looks towards the gate in front of the facility and sees a big silhouette jump across the building. The silhouette then landing in front of the gate. As the Group stares at what or who is standing in front of them, they all look in fear. An eight-foot human like Tiger, standing just a couple of feet away from them, this monster has the eyes of a Tiger. It is mouth wide open as drool runs down its face, it stands like a man with big hands and claws popping out, it looks like an abomination. The creature has blood all over its mouth, scars all over its face and bloody big teeth growling at the group. Einsberg panics as he unloads the assault rifle towards the creature missing half his shots and the ones that has hit the creature seemed to do no damage, which only makes the monster angry. The creature roars and runs towards Einsberg. The group all run and split up but Einsberg freezes. Spike grabs Einsberg out of the way as the abomination tried to tackle Henry but misses the body. Spike locks eyes with the monster standing in front of Einsberg, the monster let us out a roar towards Spike. 656 shoots the creature in the back. But it does not damage, the creature then turns his attention on 656 and charges him.

656 begins to run away while yelling out. "Hey, I will set a distraction!! Spike and dog let the doctors reach the gate; we can manage this beast come on!!"

As the abomination chases 656, 656 hides under an old jet. The Monster tries to lift the jet while Rocky and Spike run behind the monster. Spike gets the creature's attention, by jumping on the creatures' back and scratching the back of the creature's head. As the creature roars in pain, he violently throws himself on his back trying to crush Spike. Spike quickly jumped off the creatures back, doing a backflip and landing behind the monster. Rocky then jumps on the creature and bites it on the neck while the creature is still on its back. The creature lets out a horrifying scream; the monster tries to grab Rocky, but Rocky jumps off the creature's chest. Spike is behind the monster, While Rocky is staring at the creature.

Spike then shouts. "656!!! Rocky!!! Run towards the cliff side I have a plan!!!!"

656 has a lead against Rocky since he was hiding under the jet. Rocky stares at the creature then quickly runs after 656. The creature begins to chase Rocky but before it can pick up speed, Spike grabs the monster's attention by throwing a skull he picked up near him at the monster's head. The monster turns around and locks eyes with Spike. Spike and the creature stare at each other for a quick moment. Spike then begins to run in the opposite direction. Spike runs across the old jets and jumps on abandoned army tanks; he begins to head towards the other direction of the cliff side. The monster is right on Spikes' back, but Spike is incredibly fast. 656 finally stops running and Rocky catches up to 656. Both stare in the direction of Spike and the monster.

656 says to Rocky while breathing fast. "Hey Dog, your brother is going to try to make that creature fall off the cliff."

Rocky replies. "Yea I see that!!"

Spike is running as fast as he has ever ran towards the cliff side. Spike sprints fast towards the right, the monster when for a dive but nearly fell off the cliff. This time Spike, without stopping, changes his direction and begins to run towards 656 and Rocky. The monster is right behind Spike again, 656 and Rocky split opposite directions allowing Spike to baseball slide towards the edge of the cliff as he holds on to the edge of the cliff. The monster, unable to hold his speed, does not see the edge until it is too late. The creature falls to a pit of stones at the bottom of the cliff. 656 and Rocky rush over to help Spike get back up from the cliff side. The two pull Spike up to safety while they are all breathing heavy.

Rocky asks Spike. “You alright bro?"

Spike breathing heavy replies. “Yea, I’m fine just some scratches on my knees that’s all."

Einsberg and Shannon come running to help.

Shannon says. “What in god’s name was that thing!!"

Rocky replies. “I don't know but I'm starting not to like the looks of this place."

Einsberg tells everyone. “I’m sorry everyone I just froze, I- I don’t know what happened there."

Spike pats Henry on his back and says. “You’re alive, you’re well thank the lord."

Einsberg smiles and nods his head. The group begin to walk towards the gate. The entrance of the gate, 656, you sees the door that reads "Gate 2-B."

656 touches the sign and whispers to himself. “This...... This is just like my dreams."

Einsberg puts his hand on 656 shoulder and tells him. “Come let's head in."

The group heads into the base and shut the door from behind entering the so-called abandoned Science base. What will they encounter inside after witnessing an abomination just outside the facility? Will it be answers or more questions?

Chapter 13:

Explanations..........

Janjii and the other warriors along with Maxayus, remain shocked at the whale carcasses that have washed up shore. The warriors begin to mutter, at this moment Janjii snaps out of his thoughts and begins to speak.

Janjii says to everyone. "My people please, do not be alarm for we will try to search answers for why this is happening!"

A random warrior asks Janjii. "Excuse me Janjii would we be able to eat the carcasses?"

Janjii quickly replies. "Brother, we do not want to infect our flesh with whatever killed these creatures, we should be safer if we do not eat any of the whale meat. Even though we do not get ill, we do not want to Risk our luck. In the meantime brothers, please head back to your huts, tend to your women and young ones, for night has come upon us, we will discuss further in the daytime."

The warriors all listen to Janjii and begin to head back to their huts. Maxayus is the only one who stays alongside his father.

Maxayus then asks Janjii. "Father, what should we do in the morning??"

Janjii replies to Maxayus and says. "We must be patient my boy, let us see what the others will say when they return."

Maxayus raises his eyebrows in confusion and replies. "Father the others? How are you so sure they will return?"

Janjii turns towards the ocean while holding his spear and says to Maxayus. "They will return my son, they will return. You must have faith in them, they will return."

The scene then pans out and moves onto the other side of the beach. There we see Maya by the beach area, staring into the ocean while she is sitting on a stone. Maya gazes into the night sky with a look of concern on her face. Reedriake who happens to be walking by sees her and begins to approaches her.

Reedriake walks on the stones and politely says to Maya. "My lady?"

Maya turns around and smiles at Reedriake and she replies. "Hello Reedriake, I'm sorry I didn't hear you approaching."

Reedriake moves in a little closer smiling and says. "If I startled you my lady, I do apologize."

Maya laughs and tells Reedriake. "It is fine Reed; you are ok brother. Why are you out so late?"

Reedriake sits down a couple of inches behind Maya as he answers her question by saying. "Well, my lady, first I would like to congratulate you on your engagement."

Maya smiles and nods her head as a thank you.

Reedriake then continues. "Well also with all the commotion going on about the whales washing up, I'm not able to fall asleep."

Maya then takes a deep breath agreeing with Reedriake.

Maya says to Reedriake. "Yes, this is uneasy to take in, it's like the earth is dying. Things don't seem to be like they use to be anymore Reedriake everything is changing."

Reedriake chuckles a little bit and says. "Ah yes, the old days how things use to be. My lady, do you remember back then, how, when we were young, I use to always bring you flowers."

Maya begins to laugh and she says. "Yes, how can I forget. We were so young and funny, the good old days. Just goes to show you how time flies, like seagulls passing by."

Reedriake laughs and says. "My lady May I ask you something?" If I may not to be too personal, with your permission of course."

Maya looks at Reedriake and becomes a little more serious as she replies to him. "Go on Reed I approve." Maya says.

Reedriake then begins to say. "I'm curious to know how the outsider."

Reedriake clears his throat and continues. "I apologize my lady I meant to say Spike. I am curious to know, how is it that someone who just arrives on the previous island, can win your heart so fast?"

Maya, with a look of annoyance responds. "My heart belongs to that outsider you speak of, for the reason that his heart is pure and good."

Reedriake smirks and begins to rub his little beard. He smiles and looks up at Maya and says. "My lady it is I who has always been there for you, it is I who will always defend you, why can you not see that?"

Maya stands up facing Reedriake and says to him. "Reedriake my heart has never fallen for you. I always saw you as a brother of mine, please don't do this now."

Reedriake laughs manically and begins to rant. "So, your heart belongs to this outsider!!! Someone just arrives and takes your heart away just like that. Well, where is your warrior now? He is run off and left you here without a care, but I am still here Maya! I have never left and never will, yet you treat me as a brother??"

Maya yells back at Reedriake and says to him. "Spike is out there trying to find an answer to why this earth is dying! He is out there to help our people! That is why my heart belongs to him! I sensed his courage from the moment I laid eyes on him! You Reedriake! You do not dare question my heart! For it belongs to whom I want and I have already chosen!"

Reedriake smiles and puts his hands up and begins to step away from Maya.

Reedriake says while walking backwards from Maya. "Fair answer my lady, forgive me if I have insulted you. I will leave you at peace, farewell."

Reedriake disappears into the night walking away from Maya as she stares him down in frustration.

We now move locations to an undisclosed setting; the location is in a two-story house located on a small island. There we see Theodore on his laptop in an office room. His new assistant Eric Carner, a young Caucasian man in his late thirties stands behind Theodore waiting for his next task. Eric has taken Oswalds place; Eric is very timid and cowardly which is why Theodore likes having him around.

Theodore while on his laptop says aloud. "Strange, it has been about three weeks since I heard about Hubert and his team. Eric, have you heard from the base yet?"

Eric replies nervously. "Well sir I went ahead and sent some soldiers over about two weeks ago."

Theodore turns around facing Eric and says to Eric. "Ok? And? Have the soldiers responded back?"

Eric nervously answers Theodore. "Uhhh, well no sir I can't say I've heard anything from them either."

Theodore rubs his forehead in frustration and says to Eric. "Eric did you not think that something was a bit off if you did not hear from our soldiers?"

Eric Studders and says. "Well now tha, tha, that you mention it sir, ye, yes, yes it does seem a bit strange."

Theodore jumps up from his chair and yells. "Well then why am I just being informed about this now Eric!!!!"

Eric screams in fear as Theodore was going to strike Eric, his phone rings.

Theodore sits back down, clears his throat, and answers his phone. "Yes hello? Ah General Ratnier how may I be of service...... Yes, yes General do not worry we are working on it right away. Yes, I know, Hold one second General, Excuse me for a moment."

Theodore covers the phone, looks at Eric, and tells him. "Call the damn chopper! We head out after this phone call."

Eric nervously replies. "Yes, sir right away!"

Eric storms out of the room to call the helicopter. Theodore continues his conversation and the scene pans out, as we set back to Spike and his group in the abandoned base.

Chapter 14:

The Mysterious Team

As the team walk through Gate 2-B, they are all introduced to a metal double door. The double door requires an access badge to be scanned, but the scanner looks to be smashed. Einsberg begins to put his fingers in between the double doors middle line. The others Rocky, Spike and 656 begin to aid Henry by opening the double door. With the power of the four they manage to open the double door. Inside looks like a room that once resembled a lab. There is a mess everywhere, no one can see the rooms floor with how messy it is. While the men hold the doors open, Shannon walks in and grabs a two-foot pipe, she places the pipe horizontally to the top of the door. The men let go of the door and the pipe holds it in place.

The men begin to look around the room and Einsberg says. "OK everyone, any type of medical supplies like bandages, syringes and even water, just pack it in the bags. 656 if you begin to remember anything from your dreams let us know."

656 turns to Einsberg and nods his head in appreciation. The room is about six hundred square feet, the left side of the room has cabinets and desks thrown onto the ground, the right side looks to have monitors and electrical equipment lying around. The middle of the room has a long hall that leads towards another metal double door. Towards the front of the door, it seemed like someone or something, ran towards the door and started dropping items behind them as they went into the door. Einsberg tells Shannon while the others look for supplies.

Henry says. "Shannon there is no way we are going to find the right equipment to transfer the hybrids blood and convert it into Ryan."

Shannon replies. "Eins hun, I know you see what I see there's another door, it's right there."

Einsberg turns away from looking at the door and looks at Shannon, Henry then says. "We don't know what's back there, I ...I don't want to freeze up again."

Shannon caresses Henry's face as she tells him. "We have to open that door, let's tell the others so they can stop wasting time searching in this mess for supplies that are obviously not here."

Einsberg nods his head and calls the others over. "Hey fellas!"

Spike, Rocky and 656 look at Henry, Henry then nods his head and looks in the direction of the other door. The boys right away all synchronized with weapons drawn towards the door. The men begin to approach the door. Einsberg looks around the front of the door and sees another access badge scanner. The only difference with this access scanner is that it is not damaged. Einsberg looks through the mess in the front of the doorway and there he sees a badge. Luckily, he holds up the badge and shows the others. Everyone is quiet and speaking in eye contact and sign language. 656 points his pistol towards the door, Shannon holds another pipe in her hand and Rocky points his pistol towards the door as well. Spike stands on a table on the left side of the door, waiting to pounce on anyone or anything that runs out in case bullets do not stop whatever comes out. Einsberg takes a deep breath, the others begin to move the items in front of the doorway out of sight. Einsberg looks towards everyone and scans the badge. The sound of the air pressure from the door bursts into a small whisper and the double doors slide open, one side to the left, the other to the right.

As soon as it opens a man in a white lab coat raises both his hands and yells. "Please!! Do not shoot! Do not shoot!"

Shannon lowers the pipe while the others remain calm, 656 keeps his gun drawn at the man.

Einsberg says to 656. "Hey, it's ok, he's unarmed you can lower your gun."

656 ignores Einsberg and proceeds to question the man, while still pointing his gun at him.

656 says to the man. "Who are you?! What is your name!!"

The man with his hands still in the air, looking down responds. "Richardson! Walter Richardson!"

656 then asks. "You are here alone Richardson! Is anyone else here with you!"

Walter then replies. "No, I am not alone, the others are just down that hall into the next room."

656 responds. "So how did you see us coming?!"

Richardson nervously says. "We.... We have surveillance cameras outside, we saw all of you come inside the Gate. I... I was just getting ready to open these doors, then you all opened them."

656 says nothing but still holds his gun towards Richardson. Richardson slowly looks up at everyone with his hands still in the air. Spike steps in next to 656 and slowly lowers 656s hands. 656 looks at Spike, takes a deep breath, and lowers his weapon completely.

Spike then asks Richardson. "Sir, can you take us to the others please, we're here to help."

Richardson nods his head to confirm; he turns his back and says. "Yes, right this way sir."

Everyone stares at each other and continue to follow Richardson down the hall. Richardson approaches another door and scans his badge. The door opens there, the group sees three more scientists, the scientists all look in shock except one out of the three, who seems to have his back turned while sitting on a rolling chair.

Richardson announces to everyone. "Team! They found us! That beast outside is no more! We are safe now!"

The two men seem thankful and slowly approach the group. Einsberg, Shannon and the other three seem confused.

One of the men shake Einsberg hand and says. "Hello, I am Carl.... Carl Watkins."

The other says. "I'm Yang, Timothy Yang."

While showing his badge.

Einsberg is very confused and then he asks. "I am sorry, gentlemen, I am a little confused here, wasn't this place shut down? I was told."

Shannon puts her hand on Henry's chest to stop him from continuing. Einsberg looks at Shannon and begins to settle down.

The man sitting down finally shows his face as he slowly turns around and says. "That's what we wanted everyone else to think, but we never shut down. We stayed open all these years. My name is

Hubert Evans; I have been here twenty years already. Richardson here is our Rookie. Yang has ten years and Watkins has five years."

Hubert looks at 656 and smiles. 656 looks at him in an awkward manner. Hubert says nothing, he continues to smile and focuses his attention on Einsberg.

Without anyone asking he continues to speak. "We created that creature out there two weeks ago. We did not realize it would go in rage and attack us."

Einsberg confusingly asks while looking at the other scientists. "Why would you create such creature?"

Hubert stands up smiling walking towards Einsberg. Hubert puts his hand on Einsbergs shoulder and slowly pats on it. "Thank you for your service."

Einsberg looks down and realizes himself, Shannon, Rocky, Spike and 656 are all still wearing army uniforms.

Hubert continues to speak. "To answer that question soldier, which is what we do here. After we were told to hold off on the cat hybrids, we started to create other mammals."

Timothy opens a small door and out comes a fox, human-looking Hybrid. 656 raises his gun again pointing at the fox hybrid.

Timothy then yells out. "Oh no! My apologies, she has been in this room all day. I usually take her out to eat and spend time around people. Please she's no harm."

The fox-like hybrid approaches Rocky who is the closest to her. She begins to sniff Rocky and smiles at him while looking up at him.

Rocky smiles back and says. "Hey there girl, how are you?"

Timothy then says. "My apologies, she is not use to visitors, she gets extremely excited. Her name is Corea; she's one of our human/fox hybrids."

Rocky looks at Hubert and says. "A fox? So, she is not created from cat DNA?"

Timothy smiles and replies. "Why yes!! She does not speak. She is only twelve years of age, but she's really friendly."

Rocky pets Corea smiling then asks. "How long ago was she created?"

Timothy replies. About two months, we created her so Slye wouldn't be alone."

Spike then says. "Slye?? What is a Slye?"

Timothy looks up and points at the cabinets located above an experiment table. There another hybrid is laying down sleeping in the cabinet. This one looks like Corea but has a red fur rather than a beige like Corea.

Timothy then says. "Slye is the same age as Corea, he also does not Speak. We would like to teach them, but for some odd reason they seem not to learn very well."

Einsberg interrupts and says. "So, wait a minute, all of you created that monster out there. You continue to create more creatures, not only are you creating them for research purposes, but you're also keeping them around like mascots? What exactly are you all trying to ac here?"

Hubert replies to Henry and says. "We are simply just doing our job soldier; we have orders and are simply just obeying. We are, however, supposed to put these animals down after experimenting. But Timothy here got attached and that creature out there went on a rampage."

Einsberg then asks. "And whose orders are you obeying again?"

Hubert replies. "Why the same man that sent you to rescue us of course, My brother Theodore."

Chapter 15:

Secrets are Out!

The Group all have a silent moment after Hubert said his shocking announcement. Spike opens his mouth to say something; Richardson then interrupted him.

Richardson yells out. “My god!!! Theodore!! We must call him, he is wondering what the hell happened to us!!!"

Hubert laughs at Richardson and responds. “Calm yourself Richardson. The help has arrived, they will inform Theodore, won’t you now soldiers?"

Einsberg quickly replies. “Of course we will, right away."

Shannon looks at Einsberg confused, Henry shrugs his shoulders and Shannon looks at Hubert and asks him. “Doctor Evans I’m curious, why would Theodore ask you to create other hybrids?"

Hubert sips on his coffee swallows quickly and answers Shannon by saying. "Well, that's classified but seeing that you all are accompanied by hybrids, I don't see why you shouldn't know what stage 3 is."

Hubert begins to scatter through his desk, Shannon stares at Einsberg, confused. Einsberg also looks confused. Hubert then grabs a file from a portfolio and hands it to Shannon.

Hubert then says. "Theodore sent me this information; it was a question he found in another scientist's journal."

Shannon reads through the file, and her eyes become wide, she reads it and the words are familiar. It is a passage from her journal she left back at her home.

The file reads. "What if the cats aren't the only hybrids that carry a cure, what if other mammals related to the cat carry a cure, perhaps much stronger than the cats."

Shannon stares at Hubert and asks. "How did Theodore receive this information?"

Hubert nods his head and then responds to Shannon. "I apologize mam, I don't discuss those matters with Theodore I simply just obey orders."

Einsberg approaches Shannon whispers to her and asks. "Hun what is going on? Is everything ok?"

Shannon hands the file to Einsberg and whispers. "This is a page of my journal located in my lab back home Henry. No one knows about that journal except."

Shannon's eyes grow wide, Einsberg says. "What, what is it?!"

Shannon puts both her hands on her forehead and says. "Oh no Ornsworth!!!"

She then turns her attention on Hubert and says. "How long ago did you receive this information!"

Hubert turns around and begins to think. He then responds. "Wow I would say about eight years or so. This theory made us learn about different creatures. See like for example mammals like the cat, dog, fox etc. All are scavengers not predators. Now when we inject the cat hybrid into each mammal it transforms, but with predators such as Tigers, Bears and Lions etc. Their minds go into a state of rage, which causes the animal to be mindless and dangerous. The interesting part of this experiment is that the monkey has no effect to it."

Einsberg asks Hubert out of curiosity. "What do you mean the monkey isn't affected?"

Hubert replies. "Well besides being cured from the Eyidrotheria disease, as far as transformation, the monkey does not respond to it. Its DNA is too similar to ours, which by my understanding is the only mammal that does not turn."

Shannon becomes annoyed and yells out. "This is madness! Does Theodore not worry about humanity! He needs to publicly show the world that this hybrid blood is the cure, instead he is playing hot potato with each species!"

Hubert laughs and agrees with Shannon as he says. "Yes, that is mad, I agree with you one hundred percent. But Theodore has to hold his end of the bargain."

Einsberg then asks. "With whom?"

Hubert chuckles and says. "Oh my I do love a good gossip show. Well Theodore has that deal with the Russians, I'm pretty sure you all are aware we did lose the war."

Einsberg replies and says. "What does the war have to do with him not publicly coming out globally with a cure that will save humanity?"

Hubert answers Einsberg. "To regain global control soldier, to regain control. By holding on to the cure Theodore gains more of the Russians trust. Gaining the Russians trust, well that gives Theodore more control."

Rocky and Spike stare at each other confused. Since both are unaware of a war ever happening.

Hubert laughs and continues to speak. "What makes me laugh is the Russians buy into the bullshit. Theodore has enough of the cure for the whole world, but instead he only gives the Russians two percent of the cure."

Einsberg says. "What do you mean two percent? So, the Russians are aware of the cure?"

Hubert replies. "Hell yes, they know. But they do not know where it is coming from. Theodore gives only enough to help to those in power over at Russia. This gives Theodore that trust from the Russians that he is capable of world cure. But of course, in Theodore's mind you have to give a little to receive bigger."

Hubert laughs and grabs his coat as he packs his belongings thinking the others are there to rescue him.

Timothy then asks Spike and the others. "Would you all like to eat? We have TV dinners enough for everyone."

Einsberg replies as he looks at a clock located on the wall. "Yes, that would be fine, but first can you show us towards your medical supplies, we have some sick soldiers back at the base that need the medicine."

Timothy then replies. "Yes of course, the supplies are in that cabinet next to Slye. How many soldiers are sick you say?"

Eins looks at Shannon.

Einsberg then says. "Uhh about four soldiers are sick."

Timothy then replies saying. "Oh my."

Timothy opens the bottom fridge where he was grabbing the TV dinners and says. "Here take these, there are enough here for six people just in case you two get sick."

Timothy hands Einsberg six small capsules of the Remedy. Einsberg grabs the capsules that are on a tray. Einsberg places the tray gently in a zip lock bag that he grabbed from the room. Henry then places the bag inside his backpack. The microwave goes off making a beeping noise. The smell of the food fills the room. Einsberg, Shannon, 656, Spike and Rocky all become hypnotized with the smell of the TV dinners.

They all stare at each other in agreement and Rocky says. "Well, I guess we have time to eat before we all go."

Spike smiles and everyone laughs. The group sit down with the Scientist's and start to feast on TV dinners. Everyone is glad they are eating food other than fish, so a small silence fills the room as everyone enjoys the meal that is given to them.

Rocky then breaks the silence and asks. "So, you said the hybrids have to be put down after creation?"

Hubert's clears his throat and says. "Well, the ones who become uncontrollable, yes. We must tranquilize them and inject a serum which shuts their organs down. The reason why Slye and Corea here are still alive is because we didn't have it in us to do so."

Timothy adds to the conversation and says. "And I'm glad, look how happy they both are."

Watkins then replies. "You know if Theodore finds out he'll dispose of them."

Hubert clears his throat and says. "Ah yes did you all call him already? I know Theodore likes to receive updates; he must be furious that we have not reported. Now that the creature is gone, I can go in the other room outside and satellite him over."

At this moment, the group stare each other in silence.

656 looks around and breaks the silence as he takes his pistol out and yells. "Alright!!! Listen to me! We are leaving out of this place with the supplies in hand, if you try to stop us, I swear, I will kill every single one of you including those damn Fox things got it!!!"

The scientists all raise their hands in the air in fear, all except Hubert.

Watkins yells out. "Easy, easy take whatever you need there's no trouble here please!!!"

656 stares at his friends and says. "Is everyone ready? Let us get out of here now!"

The group are all heading towards the exit, while 656 watches the scientists aiming his pistol at them.

Hubert stands up, 656 points his gun at Hubert and says. "Buddy do not try it I have no problem putting one in your forehead."

Hubert cleans his mouth with a napkin and says. "656 will you really kill your old friend?"

656 walks closer to Hubert pointing his gun at Hubert and says. "How the hell do you know my number! To whom the hell are you talking? You don't know me!!!!"

Hubert smiles and says. "I know more than you think Raymond Styke."

656 then yells out. "Who the hell is that!!"

656 points the gun towards Huberts's head and Hubert responds saying. "My, my, my you really have no memory, do you?"

Einsberg stands next to 656 and says to 656. "He's fucking with you let's go!"

Hubert then yells out for the whole room to hear. "You 656 are Raymond Styke! An FBI agent who lost his beloved wife Karen Styke to the deadly disease Eyidrotheria!! You Raymond, volunteered to help us infiltrate the Russian government! Your mission was to be the first hybrid deployed to the Russians and retrieve information to us as a Spy!!! 656 stares at Hubert, serious but confused.

Spike then yells to 656. "Don't believe this guy 656, he's toying with you!!"

Hubert then yells out. "But I only tell the truth.... The Scar, the scar that runs across your head that is how we did it!!"

656 feels his head with his other hand and remembers that there is a scar located across his head, he always wondered where it came from.

Hubert no longer shouts and begins to calmly explain to 656. "Styke listen to me, as an old friend, your brain, your inner thoughts, they are still within you?!! We saved your life, you were diagnosed with Eyidrotheria as well, we transferred your Brain on to this body you now possess."

Everyone else's eyes grow wide in disbelief; all eyes are now on 656 as the room fills with silence.

Hubert continues to speak to 656. "You were the best! Top agent of your group, a skilled and smart fighter, which I am quite sure still lacks within you! We injected your human DNA into a cat, we created the hybrid, then moved his brain out and Raymond's brain in. We were successful, but you lost memory of your most inner thoughts. I was supposed to regain your memory with these."

Hubert reaches in his cabinet and pulls out two small objects that resemble jumper cables but smaller.

Hubert continues to explain himself. "Someone must have mistaken you for an experiment and you were deployed to the training base. I wanted to retrieve you my friend, but once you were given an experiment number, I lost you in the bunch. I could no longer find you in the database I only knew you by the number years later and the scar on your lip. But don't worry here, take these."

Hubert hands 656 the two objects and then explains to 656. "You must impale these two needles in your head for about 2 minutes. It may hurt a little, but you must dig deep into your brain, allowing your most inner memories to come back into play."

While everyone is shocked and listening to what is going on, Watkins is staring at the surveillance camera and yells out. "Uhh everyone!! Theodore just arrived and he is outside.

Chapter 16:

Reunion

Outside the Rocky base Theodore along with Eric arrive in a helicopter. Theodore can see from up top the base, a graveyard of jets and military vehicles.

Theodore yells out at the pilot. "Terry! Call Luther and see how far he is from the base!"

The pilot responds with. "Right away sir!"

Theodore continues to look from the helicopter; he uses binoculars to view the area.

Theodore then says. "God damn it our soldiers got ripped into pieces."

The pilot responds to Theodore and says. "Sir! The Sergeant says he can be here in thirty minutes!"

Theodore yells back to the pilot and says. "That is perfect! Fly us around the back of the island, there is another access to get inside!"

The pilot then flies the helicopter towards the back of the island. There towards the back side of Gate 2-b is a small cave in the middle of the side of the mountain. The helicopter lands right in. Theodore and Eric hop off the chopper and walk deeper into the cave. Theodore then crosses a small bridge, where if you look a little towards the east, you can see where the boats dock. Theodore stops walking for a second and stares towards the dock. He uses his binoculars to view the dock. Theodore stares at the dock for a long time, then continues to walks across the bridge. A couple of feet after the bridge Theodore and Eric approach an elevator door. This elevator can only be accessed by a card key. Theodore scans the card key and the elevator opens. This elevator will take Theodore right up to the examination room. But not where the scientists are located, instead the room is located just next to the scientists. There, Theodore will need his access key to enter the room.

Back inside the experiment room Hubert continues to explain how to use the devices to 656. "After the two minutes, this small box here, you will have to connect to the end of the needles cables."

Hubert hands the device to 656, 656 still holds his pistol towards the scientists.

Einsberg then yells out. "Which way is Theodore coming through, tell us now!!!"

Watkins nervously responds and says. "He...he's coming through the back door, behind us right there."

Watkins points towards the back of the room. There the group sees a metal door, no access badge required. Just a regular Aluminum door. Theodore will walk right through that door according to Watkins. Einsberg racks his rifle and points it towards the aluminum door. Einsberg then hands Shannon the backpack full of the cure and medical supplies.

Spike then asks Einsberg. “Hey, what are you doing? Let us get out of here!"

Einsberg replies to Spike. “We have the chance to kill this prick Spike, I say we do it right as he walks in!"

Spike replies. “Henry, I understand your frustration, but we must choose our battles wisely. Do you really think he is alone?"

Einsberg replies to Spike. “This is the man who cut your father’s hand off!! We cannot leave without killing him!!"

Spike is about to speak but is interrupted by 656 who agrees with Einsberg. “Sorry kid I’m with Henry on this one."

656 puts the devices in his side pants pocket and continues to point his pistol at the scientists. Watkins sees Corea and Slye moving towards the door Theodore is coming through.

Watkins then yells out. “Corea!! Slye!!! Get away from there!!!" The two fox hybrids run around the room. Meanwhile everyone is trying to keep calm. 656 is holding the gun at the scientists, while Watkins is trying to capture these animals.

656 turns his attention on the animals running around and yells out. “Get them calm or I'll kill them both!!"

Timothy begs. “Please do not! I am trying my best here!"

656 and Einsberg are both distracted from the group. Hubert runs over and tries to take the gun from 656. Timothy then hides under his desk, while Richardson gets on the phone.

Einsberg yells at Richardson to get away from the phone. He walks towards Richardson with his back now facing the aluminum door. 656 grabs Hubert in a chokehold and puts a gun to his head.

The aluminum door swings wide open, Theodore storms through the door, he holds his gun to Einsbergs head and says. “Drop it Mr. Einsberg!! Or I will have your brains all over this god damn floor!"

656 still holding his gun to Hubert's head yells out. "Let him go!! Theodore!! Or your brother gets laid out!"

Theodore looks over and notices Spike, Shannon, and Rocky standing behind 656.

Theodore then says. "Well, well looks like we have a little party going on here, don't we?"

656 shouts again. "I said drop it!!! Or I will blow his brains out!!"

Theodore laughs and says. "Hmm, interesting don't I have a gun to one of your friends head as well how ironic."

Einsberg yells out while holding his hands in the air. "656 shoot him! Do not worry about me!"

Shannon yells at Einsberg saying. "Henry! Stop talking crazy!"

Theodore responds to Shannon saying. "Ahh and look who else it is, my little thief Shannon, how are you, my lady. I heard you two have had your hands busy for a while with my experiments."

Theodore then turns his attention to 656 and says. "Speaking of them, you must be 656, you know you owe me a chopper and a couple of soldiers. Twelve I believe it was?"

656 replies. "Fuck you asshole! Get that gun off Eins head or your brother dies!"

Theodore rolls his eyes and says to Hubert. "Damn Hubert's you can never keep your god damn mouth shut, can you? I should let that fool blast you, right now!!"

Hubert then yells out. "Please Theo!!! I am sorry!!! Do not let me die!!"

Theodore then looks at his watch quickly and tells 656. "Alright!!! Listen!! I will let Henry walk and you let my damn brother walk, got it!!!"

656 nods his head in disagreement and says. "No way give us our man first!"

Theodore frustrated answers. "Listen, we can do this all day, or you can comply, it's your choice, I'll let him go at the same time, OK??"

Shannon yells and pleads with 656. "Just do it 656 please!!"

656 frustrated says. "Damn it Alright!!! Slowly!!"

Theodore lets Einsberg walk back slowly towards his group, Hubert also walks back Slowly towards his group. Hubert and Einsberg cross paths with each other, both men are now with their own group. But 656 and Theodore are still pointing their pistols at one another.

Theodore laughs and says. "You know you have made it exceedingly difficult for me all these years, all of you!!! You all will pay for it."

Spike walks next to 656 and whispers to him. "656 let's start walking towards the exit, but keep your weapon drawn towards him."

Theodore notices Spike and says to Spike. "I do not recognize you. Are you an experiment? Or one of those Indian hybrids?"

Theodore smiles and then says. "Or are you the one responsible for the sergeants eye hmm?"

Spike stares at Theodore, for the first time in their lives, both come in visual contact with each other.

Theodore smiles and chuckles and says. "My god are you?...... You are!!! You are James' little creation!!"

Theodore laughs hysterically and says. "Look at you my boy, you are all grown up. You know, if your father would have just stayed put after I chopped his hand off, he would have had a job with me. I only did it to show him who's boss!!"

Spike grows furious and puts his chin up and says. "Unlike you Theodore, I will not let the devil take hold of me. You will pay for your sins one day. But today is not the day for war."

Theodore laughs and says. "Wow a hybrid who believes in God, now I've seen it all."

Theodore laughs again and says to Spike. "Hmm actually, come to think of it, if it wasn't for me sharing that information with James years ago, he would've never created you, so in reality."

Theodore smirks. "My boy. I AM YOUR FATHER!"

Spike stares at Theodore and says. "No, you are not my father, but I will tell you what you are. You, you are a coward. A coward, a coward who hides in the shadows, a person like you deserves to be punished for all eternity in the depths of hell. A painful and slow punishment, oh and pay attention. If you try and cause harm to any of the ones I love, I will personally be the one to punch your ticket to hell. In the name of the lord and for the suffering of my father I condemned thee, Theodore, you shall suffer my wrath if you take peace away from the ones I love."

At this moment Sgt. Luther storms in behind Theodore and starts firing towards the others. Spike and everyone hit cover while bullets are flying their way. Einsberg fires back his assault rifle while behind a table that was flipped over. 656 is also firing at Luther and Theodore.

Einsberg yells at Spike. "Spike!!! Head to the boat with Shannon and Rocky while we take your cover hurry!!! Leave the base!!! Do not worry about us, take my bag hurry!!!"

Spike leads the way out the door with Einsbergs bag in hand, he looks back and notices Theodore is not shooting with Luther. Spike, Rocky and Shannon run out of the base and head towards the boat, they run through the landing strip. There they see the pilot of the helicopter. The pilot nervously attempts to shoot them but Rocky quickly runs towards him and bites his hand. The pilot screams and Rocky shoves him off the chopper. Shannon and Spike continue running towards the stairs and down to the boat. Rocky smashes the helicopters control system and begins to run towards the boat as well. Shannon starts the boat, Rocky jumps off and bites the rope tied to the dock with one chomp. Meanwhile 656 and Einsberg are unloading rounds, while Luther shoots back. Luther begins to reload, 656 and Einsberg make their way to the exit. They run towards the landing strip. Theodore shows up in another helicopter that Eric is driving. Theodore begins to shoot an assault rifle towards 656 and Henry. 656 quickly heads to one of the abandoned tanks, Einsberg hides under a jet. 656 inside the tank begins to operate it. 656 shoots the helicopter blades and the chopper loses control. Eric and Theodore jump off and land on the landing strip. 656 hops out the tank, while Einsberg comes out from hiding under the jet. Both men begin running towards the stairs down the dock. Gunshots fire towards them. Luther is firing still, Einsberg fires back at Luther.

Einsberg says to 656. "I see the others they are down there!! Go, go!!"

656 dives into the water from the stairs. Einsberg is exchanging rounds with Luther still. Einsberg then sees a military vehicle with a cylinder tank under, Einsberg shoots the cylinder tank located a couple feet from Luther. The tank explodes causing Luther to take cover and Einsbergs chance to flee. Henry dives into the water, 656 is also in the water. Shannon drives the boat beside 656 and Einsberg and both Rocky and Spike pull them on board. The group look back towards the base. The base is at least a mile away from them. The group all gather and compose themselves; everyone laughs and cheers while Shannon drives the boat. Einsberg reaches in his backpack which Spike returns to him. Henry takes out the zip lock bag and kisses the bag, and everyone seems relieved and happy, 656 smirks. 656 reaches in his side pocket where he still holds the

devices, he looks around and no one notices he holds the devices; he hides them back in his pocket. The scene pans out, we see the boat heading back towards the hybrid island, where the group finally heads home.

Chapter 17:

Reevaluate

Back at the experiment base, Theodore picks himself up from the landing strip. Theodore and Eric jumped off the helicopter and landed hard. Sergeant Luther approaches both men concerned, Luther sees both men are alright and feels relieved. Theodore has scratches on his knees and palms, Eric seems to have landed worse since he is limping, Eric sprained his ankle.

Luther helps Theodore up and Theodore says. “I’m fine Sergeant, I’m fine."

After Theodore begins to laugh maniacally, looking all around the landing strip, he continues to laugh uncontrollably. Sergeant Luther goes and helps Eric up and puts Eric’s arm around the back of his neck to support Eric’s balance. The three men begin to walk back towards the experiment room where Hubert and his team remain. Sergeant Luther is also a little injured with blood running down the side of his head. Theodore heads into the experiment room still laughing and rubbing his eyes. Hubert and the rest of the scientists look afraid and confused. Theodore sits on a chair near the experiment table, he asks Luther for a cigarette. Luther hands him a cigarette and lights the cigarette for Theodore. Theodore takes a hit of the cigarette and exhales the smoke in the air.

Theodore stares at Hubert and chuckles, he then says to Hubert. "Hubert, tell me something.... How did Henry know about our sibling relationship?"

Hubert takes a deep gulp and says. "I'm sorry Theo, I really believed he was one of your men sent to save us."

Theodore bangs on the table and yells. "God damn it!! Hubert why would that still make it ok to discuss our business!!! Why would anyone outside of this facility need to know that!!"

Hubert flinches in fear and the other scientists remain silent and awkward. Theodore takes another hit of his cigarette and ask Hubert. "Did you say anything else; besides we being related?"

Hubert nods his head and says. "No Theo, I didn't say anything else I swear."

The other scientists stare at each other in confusion, but none of them call lies on Hubert. Theodore looks around the experiment room while smoking his cigarette. Theodore hears a rumbling across the room and immediately jumps up with his pistol in hand. Luther takes a knife out and everyone stares towards the sounds of the rumbling. There across the room everyone sees Corea and Slye, who are chasing each other and playing. Theodore turns his head towards the scientists while still holding his pistol towards the foxes.

Theodore then asks. "What...... In.... The.... Hell... are those things!"

Richardson steps forward and begins to plead with Theodore. “Sir, please if I may, I believe Slye and Corea will make a good asset for us."

Theodore interrupts Richardson and says. “Slye and what?"

Richardson replies. “Corea, sir her name is Corea, they are both brilliant creatures and are remarkable in taking orders. The only problem we’ve had is teaching them to speak."

Theodore laughs and says. “So, you named these abominations?"

Theodore then points his gun at them.

Timothy shouts and begs. “Oh, please sir!! Please do not!!"

Hubert steps in front of Theodore and pleads with him to listen to what Richardson has to offer.

Hubert says. “Theo please, just listen to Richardson if not, listen to him for Father. Remember his promise."

Theodore sucks his teeth and lowers his gun he then says to Hubert. “Only promise I made to father was to keep you safe and not kill you myself."

Theodore stares at Richardson, Theodore says. “Alright Richardson, let’s hear your plan."

Richardson looks back at Hubert; Hubert then gives Richardson a nod of approval.

Richardson clears his throat and begins to speak. “Well sir as I was saying, I’d think they’d be a good asset to the Hybrid Bounty System, better known as the HBS."

Theodore laughs and says. “Out of all creatures, you want to make them a part of the HBS? I don’t see how this makes them an asset."

Richardson clears his throat once again and says. “They may not look dangerous, but they are faster and more agile than the cat."

Theodore raises his eyebrow turns to a sobbing Timothy and says. "Well congratulations Mr. Yang, it seems like you get to keep your pets alive after all."

Sergeant Luther signals Theodore to get his attention, Theodore walks over to the Sergeant and the Sergeant whispers to Theodore. "Sir, what about the hybrids and those scientists? Are we going to follow their trail? I saw them heading east off the island. I'm pretty sure that's the same direction as the island they live on."

Theodore smiles and responds. "Patience Sergeant, this is exactly why we have the HBS project. First let us get out of here, all of us. Second, we take Slick and Corey or whatever those abominations are called, get them geared up and lastly, we invade the island. Sounds Good?"

Sergeant Luther stares at Theodore, confused and responds. "No problem, Sir, you're the boss."

Eric approaches Theodore and says. "Sir, I apologize earlier for not being able to fly the helicopter so well, I was afraid and nervous, I do want to apologize."

Theodore responds to Eric and says. "You're a damn coward Eric!!! Which is why I keep you around, I will never have to worry about you stabbing me in my back. Now start calling for a chopper, better yet call for two, if we are going to do things we are going to do them correctly this time."

Theodore then turns to Hubert and asks. "Ahh what happened here with everything? The soldiers outside and you all having to barricade yourselves, what caused all this wreck?"

Hubert nods his head and answers. "The tiger Theo, it was the tiger."

Theodore smiles and says. "Really? The Tiger? And May I ask what went wrong?"

Hubert then responds. "He was uncontrollable with rage. As soon as we awakened him, he began to attack. Luckily, we were able to get him out of the examination room by letting out one of test monkeys. He chased it outside that gate there and we began to barricade ourselves once it was out of the room. We watched it tear all the soldiers in pieces through the only surveillance camera we had."

Theodore laughs and says. "Amazing! What strength and power!"

Theodore seems excited, then snaps back into reality and he says. "Ok everyone we are going to relocate, and we are going to begin a new project. This time I want everyone on board and open-minded with using lethal force."

Hubert then asks. "Lethal force Theo?"

Theodore laughs and says. "We are no longer going to create or experiment to analyze and learn. No, we are now going to make predators my fellow teammates, not weapons, not soldiers but instead Predators. Creatures that will hunt, stalk, and kill, this will be the main goal understood?"

Everyone says. "Yes sir."

Hubert then asks Theodore. "So, Theo what's to become of this place?"

Theodore stares into Hubert's eyes and says. "Well as far as I am aware this place is no longer unknown; it has been discovered and can no longer be secured. It will no longer be standing, I will terminate this place once and for all, where it will be nothing more than regular rocks over the ocean."

Theodore begins to tell everyone to pack up, as they await the arrival of the helicopters to come and relocate everyone in the base.

Chapter 18:

Venting and Convincing

Back on the boat the group are already one hour into sea. Einsberg has taken over the driving meanwhile, Shannon takes a nap inside the boats deck. Spike sits down just outside the deck and Rocky sleeps on the floor inside the deck. Spike notices 656 staring out into the ocean, 656 has not said a word since they escaped the base. Spike, being a concerned friend, stands up and approaches 656, standing next to him as he stares into the ocean too.

Spike says. "Isn't it amazing how we can't see what's beyond the ocean. We are just floating above its surface not knowing anything that's under it. I feel like we are all just like the ocean, we all are visible by our appearance, but no one knows what goes on inside our mind."

656 picks his head up with a serious look and says. "Every night as long as I can remember, I've had these nightmares. That gate, those tubes we saw back there, everything only to find out it has

been memories, memories of the day I became this, this walking abomination."

Spike stares at 656, turns his back towards the ocean and leans against the railing.

Spike says. "Abomination is such a strong word to use in this type of situation 656, you yourself said it just now. Everything that you believed was dreams and nightmares has just been memories. 656 I understand that you are processing a lot right now, I understand that this is something very confusing and difficult for you.

There's a lot to think about here, you have Luna, a child that is about to be born, which you are the father of that baby. God has presented to you a tool, a choice that only you can make."

656 smirks and says to Spike. "God? Out of all things you can talk about you mention God? The last thing that's in my mind right now kid is God."

Spike replies. "I mentioned God because the dreams, the nightmares these all the sudden reveals in your life. That is not something scientists created. That is not something man made. This all came from your mind, your thoughts, your memories. Abomination does not have those tools by God; abomination only has a destructive nature towards God. That man back there, Theodore. It is more of an abomination than that creature who attacked us back there. You."

Spike puts his pointer finger on 656s chest. "You are a creation of god, and god wants you to do something, I don't know what it is weather that's staying in Lunas life and being there for all of us or something more."

Spike then points towards 656s side pocket where the tools are located.

Spike then says while pointing. "That decision you make, whether it benefits you, Luna, or any of us. Just know that no matter what, someone is going to be affected."

656 holds his pocket looking down then looking at Spike.

656 whispers to Spike. "You knew I was holding on to them this whole time?"

Spike turns his focus back towards the ocean and says. "656 I want to thank you for bringing me to Maya. I also want to thank you for allowing me to face the men that once terrorized me and my father. But this choice you are going to make, all I ask of you is.... let it be a choice that will bring you closer with God. Let it be, to save you and people that need saving. All I ask is that whatever choice you make, become a warrior of God, and become a fighter for yourself."

656 stares at Spike and responds. "So, you aren't concerned for the choice I will make?"

Spike sighs and says. "By the hands of God, your choice has already been made. I'm just simply asking you to let God guide you on your journey."

Spike puts his hand on 656s shoulder and walks back towards the front of the deck. 656 stares into the floor then back towards the ocean. 656 turns towards Spike and sees Spike sitting down, head tilt back and eyes closed. 656 can't help but think to himself that Spike was saying his farewells to him.

656 looks out at the ocean again and says to himself. "That kid amazes me every day, he is a walking warrior, an angel in disguise."

656 holds his side pocket again and closes his eyes.

He then says. "Hey big man, how are you? Forgive me for not checking up on you as much. But I ask you please, give me strength and guidance on my journey you have allowed me to begin.... Amen."

Inside the deck Shannon wakes up and sees Einsberg driving the boat, she gets up with a blanket wrapped around her and walks towards Einsberg. She leans her head on Einsbergs shoulder, and he leans his head on her head while driving the boat.

Shannon whispers to Henry. "Oh Henry" she begins to cry silently and says. "Why do the good suffer the most. Why is it that people like Theodore can live so long."

Einsberg puts one arm around Shannon while driving the boat.

Henry says. "Shhh honey it's fine, don't lose faith please, we are going home no one is following us and we are going to save Ryan. Then we can all go back to the city and present the cure to everyone and expose Theodore. We're going to be ok, I promise, one day at a time hun."

Shannon rubs her face in Einsbergs shoulder crying and says. "He killed Ornsworth, Henry, he killed him because of me."

Einsberg replies. "Hey, listen to me anything that bastard has done has nothing to do with blaming ourselves, ok? Ornsworth was not your fault, Theodore will get what's coming to him, even if it means I die for it, he will be get what he deserves."

Shannon lays her head on Henry's shoulders still sobbing a little.

Rocky inside the deck also wakes up, he yawns and stretches his arms out and looks around. Rocky sees Shannon laying on Einsbergs shoulder he looks to his right and sees 656 staring into the ocean, when Rocky turns around he sees Spike lying his head against the ships deck. Rocky decides to go and check on Spike to see how he's doing, Rocky walks out the deck and approaches Spike. Spike opens one eye and smiles as he sees Rocky standing beside him.

Rocky says. "Mind if I sit down with you?"

Spike smiles and scoots over so Rocky can sit next to him.

Rocky then says. "I wonder why everyone is so quiet, you would think they'd still be celebrating after what we just accomplished."

Spike says. "I think everyone is just tired and ready to get home."

Rocky pats Spike on his head and says. "What about you? Feeling excited to get back to Maya?"

Spike looks at Rocky smiling and says. "More than anything in the world, I'm going to hug her and probably never let her go."

The boys laugh together and Rocky says. "I'm happy for you bro, I really am. I'm glad you found someone who loves you and cares about you, that's really beautiful."

Spike looks at Rocky and notices something is bothering him.

Spike asks Rocky. "Hey you ok?"

Rocky smirks and says. "Yeah I'm good bro, why do you ask?"

Spike responds. "Because you are my brother and I know you very well, talk to me."

Rocky stares at Spike and chuckles. "That sixth sense of yours is quite impressive bro."

Spike rubs Rocky's back and says. "What's on your mind?"

Rocky replies. "Well, back at that lab I was just thinking about those two creatures, the foxes?"

Spike says. "Yeah what about them?"

Rocky then continues. "Well come on Spike, you can't see where I'm going with this?"

Spike looks at his brother thinks for a moment then says. "No, I don't see where you're going with this, why don't you say it bro?"

Rocky takes a deep breath and says. "Those things have each-other bro, they are the same species and all. Male and female at that, they aren't alone."

Spike sits up and says to Rocky. "Hey, hey you aren't alone ok? You are one of us Rocky."

Rocky says. "Spike let's be realistic I'm a hybrid dog, the only hybrid dog at that. Oh, and to make matters worse I age a lot quicker than you, let's be honest I'm going to be alone, but hey I'm alright with that really I am."

Spike looks at his brother, thinks to himself, and says. "Hey, as far as I know you carry my DNA inside you, that makes you no different than me or the others back in the island you hear me?"

Rocky says. "Yea I hear you."

Spike continues to say. "As far as you aging and saying you'll be alone for the rest of your life is not true Rocky. So many of us including Morycus, Maya the doctors, we all love you. So don't ever feel like you are alone bro. You deserve to feel loved and happiness.

"Spike tears up as he talks with his brother. "Rocky I love you and there is someone for everyone, believe me you have more personality and charisma than anyone I ever came across."

Rocky laughs and says. "That's because you only have come across Scientists, hybrids and Evil Scientists."

Both Rocky and Spike laugh. Rocky then leans his head back and says to Spike. "You still think about her?"

Spike stares into the sky and replies. "Every day, not a day goes by I don't think about Rosie."

Rocky also says. "Yea me too, I wished I would've been able to speak to her like you were. Even though, my memories of her still feel nice."

Spike smiles and says. "She brought us together."

The boys smile at each other and Spike puts his right arm around Rocky he says to Rocky. "I love you bro."

Rocky replies. "I love you too bro, thanks for cheering me up.

The scene pans out with both boys looking at the ocean and the sun rising over the horizon.

Chapter 19:

Confrontations……

Back at the island, Maxayus and Reedriake are out looking through the small woods for any birds or small mammals. Both carry bow and arrows and quietly move through the woods.

Reedriake says to Maxayus. "You know this is pointless Maxayus, there is nothing out here..."

Maxayus keeps a close look towards the top of the trees and answers Reedriake. "We must still scavenge; one must not lose hope Reedriake."

Reedriake chuckles and responds. "I lost hope a long time ago my dear friend."

Maxayus replies. "Well, I hate to be the one to regain your hope brother. Look over there, towards the small bushes."

As the two look over, they see a heard of vultures scavenging the bushes. Maxayus and Reedriake both pull out their bows and arrows.

Maxayus smiles and says. "Remember when we were younger and we use to compete which one of us can hit the most coconuts??"

Reedriake grins and says. "Ahh yes I remember."

Maxayus draws his arrow at the vultures and says. "Well brother, let's see which one of us has the better aim and faster arrows."

The two start to shoot the vultures as they scatter and try to fly away. Maxayus and Reedriake are so quick, the big birds all start falling to the floor. After all the vultures have been shot down, Reedriake and Maxayus walk around and remove all the arrows. Both tie all the bird's feet and pick them all up like a sack. Reedriake with one flock and Maxayus with another, they head towards the village.

As the boys walk Reedriake laughs excitedly and says. "I think I won that one wouldn't you say?"

Maxayus nods his head in disapproval and replies. "You have grown quicker with your hands friend, but I think I still overcame."

Reedriake also nods his head and says. "Always saying you're right when wrong same old Maxayus."

Maxayus and Reedriake have finally touched sand, which means they have reached the village limits.

Maxayus happily tells Reedriake. "This shall please the village. I wonder when the others will get back, it's been some time now."

The two continue to walk Reedriake stops and says. "It has been some time now, do you not think it's selfish of Mayas love to leave her behind?"

Maxayus turns around while still holding the vultures he stares at Reedriake and says. "My father says Spike is doing it for our people. I trust my father's judgment; there is no bad feelings towards Spike."

Reedriake asks. "How is your relationship with him? Do you believe he is strong? Do you believe he is of warrior spirit?"

Maxayus nods his head as an approval and says. "He makes my sister happy, as far as what I believe in him, I sense a good energy from him."

Reedriake laughs. "I knew it! You don't see a warrior in him, all you see is he makes Maya happy. This is what I've been trying to show everyone all along!"

Maxayus raises his eyebrows and says. "Now wait a minute brother, I never said I didn't see a warrior spirit in him, what I said was."

Maxayus gets interrupted by Reedriake. "Yes I know what you said! But you must admit that Maya deserves someone stronger and knows the ways of our tribe."

Maxayus smirks and says. "Oh, and you feel as though you can be that warrior?"

Reedriake laughs. "Well, I believe that I can bring her happiness and protection. See that outsider can only make her happy, I can make her feel like a brand-new woman and treat her like a queen. She can also feel proud of calling me her king. That outsider, she's going to have to worry for him every time danger is near. With me she will never know fear."

Maxayus begins to grow upset as it shows in his face.

Maxayus replies. "I don't think you see the way my sister chooses her life. You make it seem as if she needs a protector, or she needs protection, when she has two brothers who can do this for her. See that outsider, he makes my sisters heart fill with love and joy. I've never seen her as happy as she's been since he arrived on this island. You, you consider yourself a better fit for Maya and you say it as though I have the authority to change her mind. Why is it that you speak this way of my sister?"

Reedriake picks up his vulture flock and begins to walk towards the village.

He walks past Maxayus and says. "My apologies brother, I believed by expressing myself towards you, that you'd be more understanding, but I should've known your father still has a hold of your mind and thoughts."

Maxayus replies. "What is this nonsense you speak of Reedriake? Do you have more on your mind which you seek to explain?"

Reedriake stops walking and looks at Maxayus from over his shoulder and says. "Do you not like to hear the truth? I am just stating what is said around the island. Maxayus the future chief, such a strong warrior, the only problem is he can't think for himself, he always needs his father's opinion and support to make his own decisions."

Maxayus closes his fist, he then calms down and smiles as he says to Reedriake. "I know what this is all about."

Maxayus laughs. "You are angered because my father disapproved your request for Maya to change her mind. Then you tried to pursue your idea towards Maya and she also disapproved. I can admit I do seek advice from my father but wouldn't I? He was right about something."

Reedriake then asks. "Oh and what was he right about?"

Maxayus laughs and says. "His judgment towards you, see while you made Maya feel uncomfortable that outsider won her heart. Your heart is shattered to pieces because Maya chose a warrior not for his strength but rather for his spirit. You lack both spirit and happiness."

Reedriake also closes his fist and smiles, he then replies to Maxayus. “You know Maxayus you are right, your father chose spirit over a warriors strength. But it makes sense now, since your father does not even know how to raise a warrior himself."

Reedriake laughs and continues. “Morycus is doomed to the fact that he has to gaze upon lies being told and wrong paths being chosen!"

At this moment Maxayus throws the birds down and Reedriake turns around and does the same.

Reedriake says. “Here we go, let's see what your father has taught you in combat!"

Maxayus charges Reedriake, they both locks hands in a test of strength and agility. Maxayus begins to overpower Reedriake bringing his knees to the sand. Reedriake sweeps his right ankle behind Maxayus left ankle. Maxayus falls on his left knee, and both men still lock hands while on one knee. Maxayus pushes towards Reedriake again overcoming Reedriakes strength. Reedriake quickly spins to the right breaking the grip of strength between the two. Now the boys are staring at each other face to face. Maxayus throws a punch hitting Reedriakes left eye. Reedriake begins to throw punches but Maxayus bobs and weaves every single punch. Maxayus back on his feet, walking backwards dodging, Reedriake dives at Maxayus bringing him to the ground once again. Maxayus holds Reedriakes head between his ribs and armpit Reedriake picks Maxayus up and slams him on his back causing Maxayus to release. Reedriake stands back on his feet, as so does Maxayus. Reedriake charges him again, Maxayus quickly charges towards him as well and punches Reedriake in his nose. Reedriake wipes the blood off his nose, he dives directly for Maxayus's legs and both again on the floor, the two start to wrestle around Maxayus gets on Reedriakes back and puts him in a choke hold. At this moment, a couple of warriors and Janjii come running to break up the fight.

Janjii yells out. “You two enough!!!"

Janjii separating the boys. “What is the meaning of this Maxayus!!" Maxayus wipes blood off his lip and says while breathing hard. “Nothing father, Reedriake wanted to question my strength, so I had to give him an answer."

Reedriake opens his arms while blood runs down his nose, he smiles and says. “I still question it, you coward!!"

Maxayus tries to lunge back at Reedriake, Janjii pushes Maxayus away as other warriors hold Maxayus back.

Janjii yells at Reedriake. “That's enough Reedriake, we shall discuss this matter!"

Reedriake looks at Janjii and says. “Nothing to discuss Janjii, take the food and enjoy! I'll be on the other side of the island where I belong!!!"

Reedriake grabs the flock of tied vultures and throws them towards Janjiis feet. Reedriake walks away as Janjii stares at him with concern.

Janjii turns back to Maxayus and asks. “What happened!?"

Maxayus shoves the warriors away from him and replies. “I've already told you father; it was a matter of strength."

Maxayus picks up his flock of birds and walks back towards the village. Janjii stares at his son with a look of concern.

Morning begins to overcome the sky. We now see the group on the boat getting closer to the island. Einsberg still driving, while everyone except 656 are still sleeping.

Einsberg yells. “We're home everybody!!! rise and shine!!!"

Rocky wakes up yawning. “Finally!! Aw man, I'd never thought I'd be this Happy to see an island again."

Spike smiles while standing in front of the boat. "Maya...... I've come home."

As Einsberg gets closer to the island he sees Janjii and other warriors cheering on the arrival of the group. Einsberg approaches the island letting the boat come on land. Everyone gets down to greet, 656 ties the boat to a stone in the sand.

Janjii approaches Einsberg and hugs him. "Welcome back my friend."

Einsberg smiles. "It's good to see you again Janjii."

Spike sees Maya as she runs towards him, both hug and Spike picks her up and kisses her.

Maya says. "How I've missed you, my love!"

Rocky shakes Morycus' hand and speaks. "I've missed your brother-in-law."

Morycus smirks and replies. "So have I dog breath, so have I."

Shannon hugs Stacey and says to her. "Ryan is going to be ok, I promise."

Stacey hugging Shannon with tears of joy running down the side of her face replies. "Thank you, thank you."

Luna approaches 656 who is still tying the boat.

Luna says. "Everything ok?"

656 smiles and kisses Luna as he replies. "Yeah, everything is alright."

656 rubs her belly and the group begin to settle in. Einsberg walks towards the hut where Ryan awaits his friend's arrival.

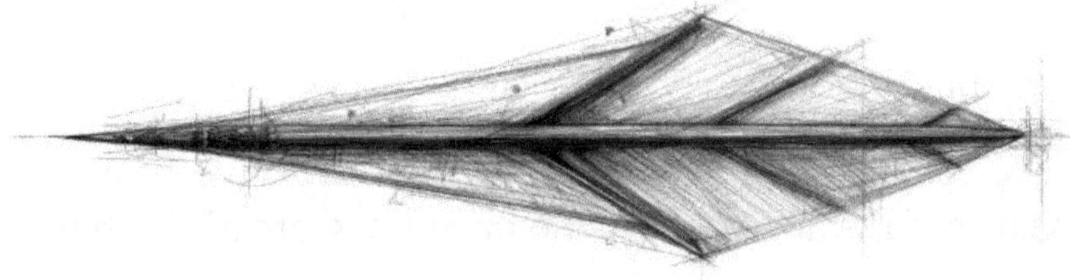

Chapter 20:

The Plan

Einsberg along with Spike, Shannon and Stacey Walk inside the hut where Ryan lays. Einsberg walks in with the backpack in hand, inside holds the six capsules in the zip lock bag.

Einsberg kneels to Ryan who is still lying down. Einsberg places his hand on Ryan's head, Ryan wakes up and smiles. "Henry you've come back."

"I'm here brother and look." Einsberg says.

Ryan opens his eyes and asks Einsberg. "What is it? Some whiskey?"

Einsberg laughs while holding the capsule and speaks. "We've found it, this is the cure."

Ryan try's his best to sit up but struggles to do so. Einsberg gently puts his hand on Ryan's chest and speaks. "Easy, take it easy."

Henry then takes out the syringes and needles from the backpack. Henry gently injects the needle into the capsule and pulls out the remedy into the syringe. Henry looks around at everyone. Shannon grabs a tourniquet and wraps it around Ryan's arm. As she does this, Spike observes everything. Einsberg waits to see the veins become visible. Henry looks at Shannon as she nods her head in approval.

Einsberg looks over at Ryan and Ryan says. "I'm ready."

Henry takes a deep breath and injects Ryan with the remedy. Henry places a small cotton onto the wound and Stacey holds the cotton. The group sit inside and wait to see what reaction Ryan has, after five minutes they notice Ryan's skin is no longer pale.

Spike becomes amazed and speaks. "Is everyone seeing Mr. Ryan's skin?"

"Yes, Spike we see it! This is amazing!" Henry yells.

Einsberg grabs a lancet and holds Ryan's hand. Ryan nods his head and Henry pricks his thumb. Shannon gives Einsberg an empty capsule where Henry places Ryan's blood. Shannon passes Henry a microscope slide to observe the blood. Henry smears the blood between two slides and uses a telescope to analyze the blood. The group watches as Henry observes the telescope. Henry smiles and laughs and tells Shannon and Stacey to look in the telescope. Both women take turns looking and both hug each-other. Spike walks over to the telescope.

Henry says. "Well take a look Spike." Spike investigates the telescope and sees Ryans blood cells fighting off the disease. It looks like the blood has overflowed with the disease.

Spike looks at the Doctors and speaks. "Our blood is capable of this?"

Einsberg smiles and replies. "Yes, Spike your blood along with the others is the cure to humanity."

Spike becomes amazed and checks on Ryan. Ryan's skin looks to be back in regular pigment, and he is looking like he's gained some energy. Spike holds Ryan's hand and Ryan smiles at Spike. We then see outside the hut Janjii standing with Maya, Rocky and the others waiting for an answer. Spike comes out of the hut and stares at everyone.

Spike says. "Everyone, Mr. Ryan is going to be ok, in fact Me. Ryan is cured!"

Everyone begins to cheer, Janjii approaches Spike and asks if he can see Ryan. Spike nods his head and Janjii steps into the hut. There Janjii sees Ryan sitting up on his leaf bed looking like himself again. Ryan smiles at Janjii, in which Janjii smiles back and gives Ryan a nod of gratitude.

Janjii steps out of the hut and ask Spike to fetch Maxayus. Spike agrees and heads to search for him.

Maya then asks her father. "Are you going to tell him the great news father?"

"Yes, my daughter, but we also have other matters to discuss as well, we must have a small meeting about how we can save others now." Janjii says.

"Others?" Maya asks.

"Yes, others my daughter, this world is dying, and we must now seek to help each person outside of our island."

Maya puts her head down and speaks. "We are going to have to relocate, correct?"

Janjii places his hand on Maya's shoulder and speaks. "I'm afraid so my daughter, it is only right as people of god, that we help those in need."

Maya seems a little concerned but says nothing. The group all settle in with the news and later that day, Janjii, Spike, Maxayus, Maya and the doctors all have a small meeting inside the medical hut. The tribe and the others await outside the hut. Finally, after a long two hours Janjii steps out along with the doctors, Maya, Spike and Maxayus. Janjii looks around as everyone grows silent and await to hear Janjiis words.

Janjii says. "Brothers and Sisters, after having a long discussion with our fellow Doctors, I believe it is best that we should relocate once more!!"

Hybrids begin to mumble. "Hear me brothers and sisters, hear me. We will have to relocate to a place unknown, not like the islands but instead surrounded by humans!"

The Hybrid mumbles get louder and one hybrid yells out. "Humans??!! Janjii what do you mean?"

"It is not safe here anymore, all of you must understand our time to relocate has come, we have no food, no room on these islands, we cannot depend on fish and coconuts any longer." Janjii replied.

The hybrid then says. "But humans??? They will not accept us??!!"

"This is a setting we must move to my fellow warriors; it is for the best." Janjii insists.

Mumbles through the hybrids get louder as they start to speak over Janjii. Janjii looks back at the Doctors with a look of Concern.

Spike then steps forward and begins to speak. "Everyone please listen this is no time to panic!!"

Mumbles become lower as silence fills the air.

"Thank you, please you must understand that this is the best choice we have. Do not fear this unknown place because it is the place I came from; this place is called Straton City. Our Blood is the

Cure to humanity; you all saw how we saved Dr. Ryan's life; we can do the same for all humans." Spike says.

"Why should we help the humans??!!" Yells out a hybrid.

"The Doctors here are humans, they went out of their way to help us, they sacrificed everything they had to bring you all here away from Theodore!!! Think of these brave humans because there are more like them out there who need us, who are dying. Children, Babies all are dying and we can stop this. By helping the Humans, we can benefit our way of living. Humans will have control of their population, which will make the earth strong again. Not only humans, but we can save everything on this planet and regain our source of food. So please, we are not forcing anyone to come with us, but we are asking for help, it is up to you to agree or just stay on the island, it is your choice." Replies Janjii.

Spike looks around, no one says anything. Spike then turns towards the Doctors and Maya. Spike holds Maya's hand and both walk towards their hut.

Maya rubs Spikes forearm and speaks. "Hey, is everything alright?"

"I just want to help everyone; we all deserve to be happy and together."

The two head inside their hut and sit down on the leaf bed.

Maya then asks. "What happened in that place you were?"

Spike looks at Maya seriously and speaks. "I met the man who made my father's life a living hell. I did nothing to avenge my father either....it just bothers me that...... Well ah never mind."

Maya hugs Spike and speaks. "Remember do not seek avenge, leave it to god my love."

Spike puts his forehead with Mayas and speaks. "It is a challenge to protect those you love, especially when there is so much wickedness that challenges you."

Rocky Comes in slowly as he approaches Spike and Maya, he clears his throat as a way of excusing himself.

Maya says. "Hello Rocky come, come you're fine."

Rocky smiles. "Thank you, Maya......the Tribe all have agreed to relocate. Janjiis discussing a plan now."

"Really??" Spike replies.

"Yea come on!!" Rocky says excitedly.

As Spike Rocky and Maya head outside, Janjii and Einsberg are letting the tribe know how they are going to travel.

Janjii is saying. "It will be a total of three trips, we will start with the women and children, then we will return for Mr. Ryan and the rest of the Doctors as they need to fit Mr. Ryan's resting bed on the boat, last we will return for the rest of the male warriors!" Ryan begins Walking towards the crowd from his hut limping. Einsberg rushes to help but Ryan denies the help.

Ryan then stands next to Janjii while the hybrids watch. "No Janjii please come back for me last, this will give me enough time to rest. I want everyone to be together with their wives and children. Take the male Warriors on the second run then come back for me last."

Einsberg then says. "We can't leave you alone I'll stay with you!!"

"No!! You are the only male, who can drive the boat just leave me alone, I'll be fine." Ryan insists.

Janjii tells Einsberg. "I'll stay with him it's fine."

“I don't want to leave you two alone like this, what if Theodore comes looking for us while we are making the trips, you will need help to fight." Einsberg demands.

“I'll stay with them!!!" Everyone looks for who said that comment and see is no other than Reedriake.

Maxayus looks towards Reedriake with a serious look. "No!!! I'll stay with my father and Ryan."

“Maxayus no!! You must stay with your mother and brother."

Janjii demands, Maxayus ignores Janjii and says to Spike. “Spike you stay with my father-"

“No!! He must stay with Maya; I want Rocky to leave with the women and Children and I want the rest of you to leave on the second trip to be with your loved ones let Reedriake stay with us!!" Janjii yells.

“I don't trust him!!!" Maxayus screams.

“Please Maxayus let me show my apologies for all I have caused, let me make it up to your family old friend.... please??" Reedriake pleads.

Maxayus gives Reedriake a serious look as he neglects his apology.

Maxayus then steps to Reedriake inches away from his face and speaks. “You better let nothing happen; you hear me!!??"

Reedriake nods his head. “You have my word old friend."

Maxayus turns away and begins to walk back towards his hut. Janjii grabs Maxayus arm, but Maxayus brushes his father off. Janjii and Maxayus stare at each other for a while but none say a word. Einsberg continues to go through the plan with the others in the background. Janjii stares at his eldest son who walks angrily back towards his hut.

Chapter 21:

A Written Letter

Sensei Ronald Brim: Mayor Of STRATON CITY.........

"Before I ran for office, I was a normal hard-working man. The community within the city knew me as a jujitsu expert and teacher. I taught many people's children and even children's parents. I was loved all around Stratton city, So I decided to run for Mayor when the city's population started decreasing. Throughout my life, I've always watched my father work hard to achieve his own goals. I grew up learning the same way, I used to work as a mail carrier, then I was promoted to managing the post office. Since I was a child, my father put me in Karate class where I learned Jujitsu. I had the same Sensei since I started, his name was Yuri Torioshi. As I became an adult and working in the post office, I still trained and brought my daughter Rhonda into it as well. My wife Wilma knew how much I loved Jujitsu and she knew how much I hated the post office. So, with my wife's encouragement, as soon as I saved enough money to open my own dojo, I did, with the blessings of my Sensei of course. Sensei Torioshi taught me everything I know, from defending, to skills in weapons and even life lessons. Hell, he's been my teacher since I was six years old. I opened my dojo and sensei Torioshi closed his, for him to finally retire and help my business grow. He said to me.

"Ronald, I see great future in this dojo, not only do I see hope, but I sense a different type of embodiment of students here as well."

I never understood that last part, knowing sensei he just said these things to boost up my confidence. This all happened before the disease first hit, I remember seeing the broadcast like it was just yesterday, the news reporter said.

"This is SCN reporting with an emergency broadcast, we still don't know what the cause for Eyidrotheria is or where it came from. Only information we have is that it started in England. We are losing more of the population, and our government still has no answers. Our Medical Scientists are working hard on a cure but have had no breakthroughs."

Ronald speaks again. "That was just the first broadcast of the pandemic, then as months went by the broadcasts would get worse, I started to hear things like."

"Meanwhile more orphanages are opening due to the children losing their families, the hospitals need more nurses and doctors. There has been word of new Hospital locations opening up as well, please everyone, our government has issued everyone to try and stay indoors, for you and your family's own safety, thank you, this has been SCN with today's emergency broadcast back to you Patricia."

Ronald again continues. "At first it wasn't a big deal to me since we have dealt with a pandemic before. But then I received a phone call, the first phone call that made me realize this was not any ordinary pandemic. I was told by Sensei Torioshis family that he has passed away due to the Eyidrotheria disease. This broke my heart, as I became very emotional throughout the next couple of months, I made a memorial of Sensei Torioshi in my dojo and I was given his samurai sword by his family, it was on his will, that I would be the one to receive this sword. It was an honor to receive such gift, and I keep it with me everywhere I go. As months turned into years, I noticed that City Hall began losing staff very rapidly, I've had to visit City Hall many times, I would always set up meetings with them to renew my business license and permits for my dojo. I was very well known in City Hall and one day a secretary told me there that they are looking to appoint a new mayor. At first, I laughed and took it as a joke. But after realizing how much the city was suffering and how much of a difference I can make, I finally decided to run for Mayor of Straton City. Being as I was born in this city, and everyone knew who I was, I had some help with the community and my dojo students to help set up a campaign for me. Maria was my secretary in charge and Arnold was my campaign manager. Both did a hell of a job getting me in office. But I must say I did take matters into my own hands when it came to the speech that got me in, since I really wasn't feeling the speech that was set up for me anyway. I told the city in my own words."

"Many of you know me as the Ju jitsu instructor. But I am here to tell you that if I am elected as your new mayor, I will get a word from our government!!! I will fight for every one of you here, like my own family depends on it. Not only will I get this city's hope back, but I will also restore everyone's spirit. Yes, we lost many friends and family members, but we cannot let this disease win!!!!! As your new Mayor, I will travel to the white house myself and I will get the answers we all deserve. I will not stop until I meet with every single scientist and find some type of breakthrough. If I must put a lab-coat on myself, I will. If you are all wondering why I'll go beyond you all. It's because I love my city, it is because of every one of you, that I am the man I am today....... So please let's make a difference, let's get some answers, and help me help you!!!!!"

Ronald speaks. "I remember being nervous because at that moment, it was silent for about five minutes, then all the sudden someone starts to clap and everyone else follows.

Two months later, I won the people's votes and became Straton City's new and first Black Mayor. Everything started off good, though we were still in the pandemic. I did manage raising a fund to help those whose families have died, I also had famous athletes as part of a fund raiser to spend time at the orphanage. I even convinced one of the Senators to visit Straton City, to talk about how hard the government is finding a cure. But as the first year of me running for office was ending, again people began to lose hope. I couldn't get a hold of the president or any government official anymore, I tried calling in fund raisers, but by the third year in office, everyone around the world was giving into this disease. No one was raising money and no one cared anymore, my election speech died along with the world we are living in now. I owe my life to my loyal and devoted bodyguards, who I've trained and worked with for years and years. I love each one of my men, they do not work on salaries and refuse to take any payment, all they ask for is to continue training in my dojo. It fills my heart with joy that some people still have a good heart during dark times. I now must mention the second phone call that made me remember what Eyidrotheria is capable of.

My wife Wilma called me not too long ago, it feels like yesterday, but it's only been two weeks. She said to me while crying on the phone."

"It's our baby Ronald, the disease......it has her now, our baby she's.......she's not going to live long."

"I stared at my phone motionless, all I could say to my wife was, where she was. As her crying words said."

"Straton City hospital.... Rhonda is in bed, she can't speak right now, we are in room 411 on the fourth floor. I'm sorry to call you like this hun I'm sorry."

"I said to her do not to apologize and I rushed to the hospital. As I jumped inside my truck I turned towards my dash, where I keep a picture of my family, there I lost it, when I saw Rhonda's face in that picture along me and my wife looking so happy, I lost it. Why God, take me.... take me, but leave my baby girl alone, not her God, she has too much to live for, she is only sixteen. My men, my bodyguards, they stand outside my daughter's hospital room every day, while I still try and manage to complete my duties as mayor. Whenever I visit her, we all always say a prayer, followed by a Japanese prayer we all learned from sensei Torioshi. But the reason I'm writing all of this, the reason I am putting everything about myself on this sheet of paper is because I have lost faith, I have lost confidence. I have lost everything I once believed our country could save us from, which was honor. I feel like this world has let me down, the people, the government, everything. It is like the entire world has given up on one another. This is no longer a new world; this has become an old world. There are no more rules, no order, no sympathy. Everything that has happened since Eyidrotheria has made this world cursed, so I am writing this letter as I sit here in the Straton City forest, looking towards the ocean located in the back of the woods. If anyone reads my letter in hopefully in a brighter future, I want you to know who I was and how we all suffered, here in Straton City. To the future of this city if you read this letter, please do not ever give up hope, fight for what is yours and never give up. Farewell to whom it may reach, I will now go spend the last days of my daughter's life with me by her side until the very end. Sincerely yours,

Ronald T. Brim"

Ronald places the letter in a small scroll; he then puts the scroll in a bottle. Ronald opens a chunk of an Oak tree bark; he places the bottle in the tree and uses some sap to seal the chunk of oak back to the tree. Ronald then grabs a small tanto blade and ties a red ribbon to the tantos handle. He stabs the area of the sapped chunk of oak; the red ribbon has a writing which says. "To the future of this city." Ronald walks into the forest and he heads back towards Straton City.

Chapter 22:

First Trip

Back on the island 656 is in his hut looking at the devices that were handed to him by Hubert. Luna walks in and finds him in a trance looking at the devices. Luna clears her throat, 656 stares at Luna but says nothing.

Luna says. “Hey, I'm leaving now, they want women and children first. Rocky will be coming with us to keep us safe."

Luna stares at the devices then locks eyes with 656, Luna then says. “Are you.... What...... do you need anything?”

656 quietly replies. “I’m fine."

Luna sits beside 656, she looks around the hut and sighs with a deep breath following then she says. “Hey if you’re not going to be honest, I am, ok?"

656 stares at her with an eyebrow raised.

Luna then says. "656 listen I want you to be happy I really do. These last three years with you on this island have made me see, the type of man you are, how you take care of me and the things you like and what makes you laugh. But honestly, I still do not know who you are. If we can just cut the bullshit already and call this what it is."

"I don't understand, what do you mean Luna?" 656 asks confused.

Luna stares at 656 and speaks. "656, I am not stupid and I am not going to sugarcoat anything, we both came from the same place. That base, that military hellhole, which taught us nothing, but guns, ammo and training let us be real with each other. I do not know how to love someone, yes, I have love for you, you are the father of this baby. But let us be honest, since we've been here, we both have been so cold and motionless for one another. We aren't Shannon and Einsberg or Maya and Spike. I feel like our hormones got the best of us and...... well shit happened!"

Luna starts to tear up. 656 puts his hand on Lunas thighs and gently rubs her thigh.

656 says. "Woman I have love for you too and this is exactly why my hormones were crazy for you."

Luna laughs and 656 continues speaking. "I want you to know something, yes, we aren't the couples of the century, but that's why we aren't who we are. We are as real as they come, Luna your honesty is the reason why I fell for you and yes you are right, that place did not teach us love, yet we found it here. So now I'm going to be real with you, why do you tell me this now and let's keep this honesty going please."

Luna cries and laughs a little, she looks up with her hand over her mouth, she then says. "Because I want you to be happy, I want you to know that no matter what decision you make, I just want your happiness that's it. I want you to know that I am going to be ok if you lose your love for me and I want you to know that I'm going to be okay if you come back to me."

Luna points at the devices and speaks. "Those things are going to give you back a memory of a life you had before you entered that base, those things are going to give you back a memory of things or someone you loved in a previous life. I want you to know that no matter what you decide, I want you to be happy."

656 holds Lunas hands and speaks. "Listen to me I'll throw those things in the ocean right now, I don't care, I'll raise our child and forget about everything, I can see what medications I can take for these nightmares and-"

Luna interrupts 656 by putting her fingers on his lips, she says to him. "Enough running away from who you are, those people took your life, but you now have an opportunity to get it back. I want you to be happy, listen to what I am saying, YOU-NEED-TO-BE-HAPPY. If you still feel like me and you are meant to be, I want you, all of you, the real you to come find me, if not that is ok because I need you to be happy."

656 sheds a tear and hugs Luna he says to her. "You are one hell of a woman, I hope to come find you, after I find myself."

Luna smiles as she hugs 656 and speaks. "You are one hell of a man, and I hope you find what you are looking for."

656 smiling says. "I'm going to remember you breaking up with me on an island by the way."

Luna laughs and stares at 656, both stare at each other and share one last passionate kiss. Luna stands up and 656 kisses her belly, Luna begins to walk towards the exit of the hut. She turns around to see 656 staring back at her, Luna does a peace sign with her fingers and 656 does the same, he then blows a kiss with his hands, Luna smiles and walks out the hut where 656 stays and stares at the devices while holding them in his hand. Outside the hut Luna walks towards the boat where Einsberg is on board ready to take the women and Rocky to Straton City. Einsberg has informed the others that they will reside in the woods of the city while figuring out how to inform every one of their whereabouts.

Janjii is talking to his wife Malaya before she boards the boat. "Be safe my queen, we shall reunite soon........ You have been a wonderful mother and wife may my spirit be with you always."

"You will be with us shortly my king, do not speak as if you will never see us again." Malaya replies.

"I love you." Says Janjii as he smiles and kisses Malaya's Hand.

"I love you." Malaya replies.

Luna smiles as she overhears their words in the background. As Rocky hops aboard the boat helping the women and children, he sees Luna with a worried look on her.

Rocky says to Luna. "Hey, we'll be fine it's just a two- and half-hour trip, we'll be there before you know it."

Luna smiles and speaks. "Thank you Rocky, you are so kind."

Rocky smiles and speaks. "Don't worry second trip you and number guy will be together again."

Luna frowns and quietly walks away.

Rocky stares in confusion and says to himself. "Sometimes I got to just stay quiet."

As the last child boards on the ship, the women, and children all wave goodbye to their fathers and husbands as the boat departs to Straton City where a new beginning awaits the Hybrids.

Rocky walks over to Einsberg as Henry drives and asks. "So, what's the plan when we get to the city Einsberg??"

"Well first we will set up in the woods where you will stay with the women and children. Since I will go back to get the men you must stay hidden from anyone and everyone. I should be back on the third trip with Janjii, Ryan and Reedriake. Ryan needs his stretcher to rest, as we will need him to show the other humans he is cured and as we do this, we will reveal the hybrids to the world."

Rocky then replies. "That's a hell of a plan... sucks that Ryan and Janjii wouldn't fit the third trip we could just leave Reed behind."

Rocky smirks after saying that, but Einsberg turns to Rocky and replies. "No one stays behind we are all family Rocky, always remember that."

"Yea, yea, I know, I'm just saying, I don't blame Maxayus for not trusting the guy he's kind of an asshole."

Einsberg then tells Rocky. "Reedriakes had it hard, his mother died during his birth and his father drowned while fishing one day out in the ocean. He's been on his own for the longest, maybe since he was 16 but he is a strong warrior and he is helping out and agreeing to stay behind benefits us."

Rocky rolls his eyes and speaks. "I guess...... How far along from the city are we?"

Einsberg checks his Compass and adding with his fingers. "About another hour and a half. I might rest up after the second trip when I head back to get Janjii, Ryan and Reed then arrive here with everybody."

Shannon and Stacey walk over to Rocky and Einsberg.

Shannon says to Rocky. "We need to stay together as soon as we get there, we have to make sure the children don't run off."

"Got cha, no problem." Rocky says.

Rocky then looks at Stacey as he notices her fidgeting.

Rocky asks. "Ms. Stacey, are you okay?"

"Yes, I am fine, I just hope Ryan will be ok on the boat. "Stacey replies.

Einsberg puts his hand on Stacey's shoulder while driving with the other hand and speaks. "Don't worry, that stretcher will hold him tight, we need him to rest as much as he can before we head out."

"I've never seen a boat this crowded before." Shannon says.

"Yes, I know, we barely got space at all, this is why I need 3 trips, there are more males than there are women and children." Einsberg replies.

Einsberg pauses for a second then talks to himself aloud. "Soon real soon, things will be good, it might be a big change for the hybrids, but it will be for the best you will see."

Shannon replies. "I know, I always knew everything will be good when you say it."

Shannon holds Einsbergs hand.

Einsberg then says. "I know one thing for sure, as soon as I make this third trip back, I am getting rid of this beard!"

Shannon smiles and rubs Einsbergs beard. "I've gotten used to it; I'm going to miss it."

"Hey, what about the guns Einsberg?" Rocky asks.

"I'll keep a Rifle with me, you take half when we depart, and I'll take the other half on the boat just in case." Einsberg replies.

Rocky says. "Cool sounds like a plan!!"

After two hours of sailing, Einsberg finally gets to the city, but instead of heading towards the dock, he drives the boat towards the woods located on the other side of the city behind the mountains. He docks the boat as everyone hops off, Rocky helps the children depart the boat, Einsberg hands Rocky the little ones that cannot reach the ground, as the last child hops off the boat, Einsberg sets sail towards the opposite side and back towards the island. The women and children wave goodbye, Einsberg departs, he blows a kiss at Shannon and waves back at some of the children who run towards the boat, but not into the water. Einsberg is now going back to pick the males up from the island and bring them with their women and children.

Einsberg says to himself. "Four more trips and everyone will be in their new home. We can reveal the hybrids to the world. Show everyone Ryan is cured by their blood and put Theodore to shame and maybe in jail."

Einsberg Looking towards the sky talks to God. "I've never talked to you, but please guide me towards safety and forgive my sins, I need you now more than ever."

Chapter 23:

Identity.........

Back on the island, every male is sitting around a bonfire as night fall hits the sky. Everyone is just quiet, not saying a word, Spike sits next to Maxayus who is across from Reedriake and Reedriake sits next to Morycus, who is burning a small fish on a stick into the fire. Morycus stayed behind due to his age and of course, proving to his father and brother that he is not child. Maxayus keeps his eyes on Reedriake which Spike is aware of. Reedriake on the other hand does not stare back but continues to sharpen his hatchet using a small knife. Janjii then walks over with a few fish he found on the other side of the island.

"Eat my brothers, eat... you must have your strength when sir Eiensberg returns."

"Father let me stay here with Reedriake and Sir Ryan, then maybe you can go to mother." Maxayus insists.

"Maxayus enough, we have discussed this already. I need you to stay with your mother and brother. Spike needs to be with Maya and that's final."

Maxayus stands up and raises his voice at Janjii. "You are mad!! You mean to tell me Spike must stay with his wife, but you must not be with mother!!!! Forgive me father, but for the first time, I question your decision!"

"Listen to me my son, you must be mature about this. One day, you will take charge of this tribe and one day, I will not be here to guide you." Janjii says.

"I have no wife, no child!!! Let me stay to show you, I can do good on my own!!!" Maxayus yells.

Janjii stays calm and speaks. "It is not about doing good on your own my son, it is about you doing excellent without me, son. I have always been there for you. Times when you hunted, I trained you to fight, this will show your true strength my son, it will show you how to guide yourself. My words are not always wise, but my ways will always be within you my son and that is what becoming a man is about. Finding your own ways and your own words, do not live by anyone else's standards, create your own boy, create your own."

Maxayus calmly but frustrated says to Janjii. "You have not made any sense since we decided to leave father, you talk as if you will never see us again, you speak madness, why now, why guide me in this way now?"

"My boy as chief of this tribe it is in my nature, that I be the last to leave the island. My son, you must remember when we moved at the previous time, I was the last to leave that island. It is a new world we are moving to, and you will have to learn it as well as I will. But one day I will not be able to teach you a new world, that even, I'm not familiar with and this is something you must teach yourself." Janjii explains.

“Preposterous you speak madness, I still don’t understand!!" Maxayus grunts.

Morycus stands up and yells at Maxayus. “Enough Maxayus!! That is enough! Father has said his peace, let it be!!"

Maxayus stares at Morycus but says nothing.

Maxayus excuses himself. “I will go for a walk around the beach; I will not be far."

Maxayus walks away from the group. Morycus walks towards his brother, but Janjii stops him and speaks. “No, my boy, let him be please, now eat the fish, go now get your strength."

Morycus sits next to Spike now taking Maxayus spot. Spike stares at Maxayus as he disappears into the night, walking towards the beach. He turns back across Reedriake, he sees Reedriake with a smirk across his face. Reedriake then looks up and sees Spike looking directly at him. Reedriake then changes from a smirk to a serious look as he continues to sharpen his hatchet and slowly looks away from Spike.

Back at 656s hut, we see 656 still with the devices now set on his palm tree bed, just staring at them, he looks like he has not gotten any rest whatsoever.

He begins to talk to himself. “Every nightmare, every memory that caused me confusion...... This whole time it was actual events that happened in my life... All this time, I never knew why I existed, where I came from or who I was.... These gadgets hold the information I seek; they hold my true self deep within.... But why hide these emotions or my ability to know certain things......I must know what the real purpose of my agreement is to be in this body.... So many years of nightmares, confusion, coming to this island. I believed I would be free.... But it still did not please me, why in the hell do I go through this!!!! Why!!!!!"

656 Starts breaking the inside of the hut down, he falls to his knees and looks up to the ceiling and yells. "I know, I know, you want me to be miserable right!!??? Is that it!!! Is that it!!! Well...... no......I will not!"

656 Walks over to the devices and grabs them, he looks back at the ceiling and yells. "This is what you want right!!! This is what you want!!! Then here, I will do it!!!!!"

656 grabs both devices and take off the capsules. The capsules come off to what looks like two sharp plugs. 656 jams one plug in his head, it goes right through, not so deep since the needles are only about two-three inches. 656 then looks at the other plug while on his knees and jams it on the other side of his head. Then 656 connects the end of both devices to the small box which looks like a battery. The shock starts running through his body like an electric chair. 656 starts to scratch the sand floor holding a ball of sand in his hands as this is happening, his mind starts to go through a roller coaster of memories. He sees himself with Luna, he sees when he first met Spike and Rocky, when he escaped to the base down to where he spoke with Exp.210 and even confronted Sgt. Luther. But then he sees a woman, a human woman, as she looks at him smiling. He then sees her in a hospital bed, then he is looking at a plaque in a cemetery with the name Karen Styke. His thoughts move forward showing a doctor's note reading. "Raymond Styke" saying this person assessed positive for Eyidrotheria. He then sees Team Adrenaline, he sees Joanne, Wallace, Cooper and even Jester. There is even a moment where it looks like he's had a love affair with Joanne. Then he sees Dr. Hubert shaking his hand, he looks to be in a room, his mind then changes to him in a restroom, where he looks in the mirror and sees a man with a soldier uniform staring back at him. The name on the Uniform says. "Styke" after, he sees Hubert with a surgeon mask, he then sees himself watching Hubert and other scientists, through a tube full of water. After all this we come back to 656, he is in a fetus position back on the island. The devices fall off his head, 656 starts to cry like he never cried before.

656 yells frantically. "Karen!!!!!! Ahhhhh!! Why!!!!! Please Karen, come back to me!!!!"

He cries while he says. "I know now, I am not 656, I am Raymond Styke!!Luna!!! I do not feel the same it......it feels different but why??? Oh no, I must get off this island now!!! I must find Hubert and avoid running into Luther and Theodore."

656.... Raymond begins to pull himself together while panting and breathing heavily.

"I'll have to wait for Einsberg, then flee when I get to the city. I must remain calm, so no one notices....... I'm sorry Luna, I'm sorry Spike, but I must get more answers. I cannot just continue to live this life, not after everything I know."

Raymond begins to think but still shaking, he bites his nails and he's sweating like a sauna.

He then says to himself. "Hubert has my documents and all my information. I remember Theodore planning to Compromise with the Russians. I was supposed to be the reason why the Russians will give up some power."

Raymond breathes and repeats three words to himself. "Infiltrate, Extract, and report. Infiltrate, Extract and report!! Damn it!!! I haven't reported it!!! Everything happening now, they must not come to an agreement, it will start a war. I must leave as soon as possible. Damn it!!!!! How the hell am I going to get to Hubert!!"

Raymond starts to think as he finally stands up and he tells himself. "I'll figure it out after I set foot back to the city. I'll get transportation and head back to the abandoned base, hopefully Hubert is still there."

After a couple of hours, Einsberg finally shows up to the island. He fills the boat with some fuel located in the boat's cabin. Janjii offers him some fish and coconut water since Einsberg looks tired.

Einsberg then walks over to Ryan's hut where he lays down. “One more trip buddy and we are back in civilization how are you doing?"

Ryan replies. “Good, good I can't wait I'm still a little tired."

“Rest up it’s going to take a while before you get all your strength back. Hey by the way, when we get back you owe me a drink." Einsberg says.

“Yea OK” Ryan says laughing.

Einsberg smiles and speaks. “Alright brother, I'll see you in five hours take care, Love you man."

“Love you too brother, be safe." Ryan replies.

Einsberg quickly rushes back towards the boat, he sees 656 rushing towards the boat as well and speaks. “Hey, you are feeling better I see!"

“Yea, yea how long till we get to the city!?" Raymond quickly asks.

“Wow easy about 3 hours.... You excited to see Luna huh?" Einsberg says.

Raymond stares at Henry and replies. “Yes, now let's go! Everyone is already on board!!"

656 jumps on the boat and squeezes through everyone.

Janjii approaches Einsberg and speaks. “Thank you, sir Einsberg, you have once again saved my people."

“No Janjii, our People." Einsberg says.

Janjii smiles at Einsberg and speaks. “Yes, Our people."

Janjii pauses then says. “Sir Einsberg may you please give this to Maxayus?"

Janjii hands Einsberg his blue coral necklace and continues to speak.

“Maxayus always loved this necklace since he was a boy."

Einsberg asks. “Why don’t you give it to him, I’m sure he’s here on the boat somewhere."

“He is not on speaking terms right now, this journey has him a life on the edge, please do me that favor." Janjii asks.

“Sure, I'll give it to him." Einsberg says.

Janjii then says. “Tell Morycus to be who he wants, not who he is told to be, please and thank you."

“Sure.... OK, I will see you soon Janjii." Einsberg replies.

Spike walks by Einsberg as he heads towards the boat, Spike walks to Janjii and Janjii smiles at him.

Spike says. “OK Janjii, we'll see you soon. God bless."

As Spike is about to hop on the boat Janjii says. “Despite how your father was Spike, you have learned much, by not making his mistakes, yet you have learned to adapt to the good he's taught you."

Spike smiles and speaks. “Thank you Janjii."

“You will be a great father someday, always remember to guide the young ones, even when they don’t listen or become stubborn.” Janjii shouts.

Maxayus is watching from the crowded boat as he listens to Spike and Janjiis conversation.

Spike replies. “Yes Janjii, I will, thank you."

“One last thing my boy." Janjii says.

“Maya is very lucky to have you my boy and you will always have my blessing, and my heart goes to you both, here take this."

Janjii takes off his bracelet. “Give this to her, she always adored it when she was a young girl, tell her she is a queen every time and love her forever."

Spike holds the bracelet in his palm, he looks at Janjii and speaks. “I will, thank you Janjii."

Spike puts the bracelet on and hops on the crowded boat. Janjii sees Morycus on the boat waving at him, Janjii removes his headband and signals Morycus to catch it. Morycus stands up on the boat ready to catch it, Janjii throws the headband and it lands in Morycus palms. Janjii waves goodbye as the boat begins to depart. Maxayus looks back towards the island where he sees Ryan, Janjii and Reedriake. Ryan is standing outside his hut waving. Reedriake is in front of Ryan just staring and Janjii is in the water, waist high, with his eyes closed like he's praying.

Maxayus says quietly. “I love you father, till we see each other again may you come to us Safely."

Chapter 24:

Distances.......

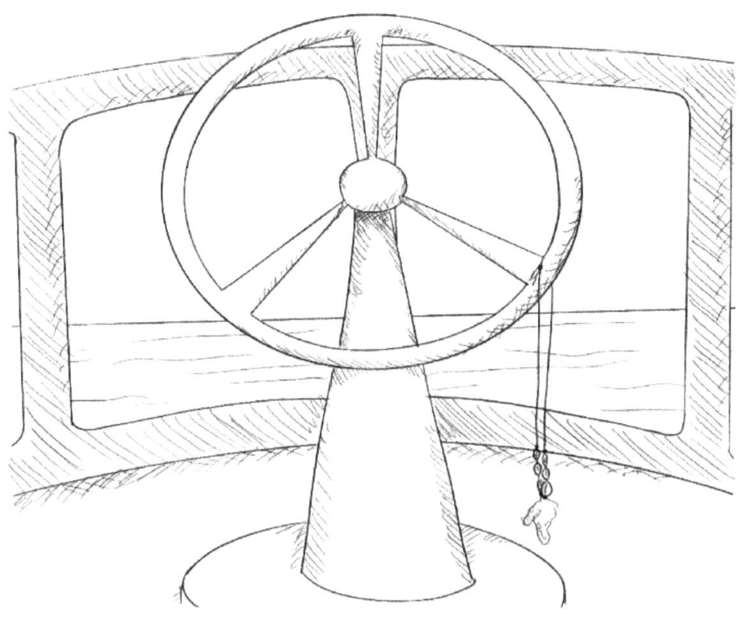

The crowded boat has already sailed for almost three hours now. The boat is so crowded, that some of the male hybrids hang a little over the railings.

Einsberg shouts at everyone. "Land!!! We are near everyone!!!" The males all shout in celebration. Raymond remains hidden within the crowded boat and has not said a word to anyone, not even Spike. As everyone gets closer, the women, children and Rocky all stand shoreline waving down the approaching boat. Einsberg slows down as he approaches the forest shore and throws the deck rope to Rocky. On the shoreline there are many stones, Rocky ties the rope tightly around one of the stones to create mooring. Einsberg has the boat facing south so after the men dock, he can easily turn the boat west and head to pick up Janjii, Ryan and Reedriake.

Einsberg remains in the deck as he watches all the men jump off, Maxayus passes by Einsberg and Einsberg quickly says. “Hey Maxayus!"

Maxayus turns towards Einsberg. “Yes, sir Einsberg? What is it?"

Einsberg pulls out the blue coral necklace from his side pocket and hands it to Maxayus. “Your father wanted me to give this to you."

Maxayus holds the necklace in his palms, he looks at Einsberg in disbelief then chuckles. Einsberg then gets distracted when he sees Spike walking by, Einsberg calls for Spike. “Hey Spike!"

“Hey Mr. Einsberg." Spike replies.

“Listen Spike thank you, if it was not for you, we would’ve never thought to migrate to Straton City, I just wanted to say thank you. Oh, and despite the way you showed up in our lives, I truly appreciate you."

Einsberg extends his hand out to Spike and Spike shakes Einsbergs hand with a small hug.

Spike whispers to Einsberg. “Let God keep you safe on your final trip, come back to us Safely.”

“Amen." Einsberg says.

While Spike and Einsberg have their moment, Maxayus places the necklace inside the steering wheel of the boat. Maxayus then hops off and begins to greet everyone on the land. Morycus runs towards his mother Malaya and quickly shows her the headband Janjii gave to him. Malaya smiling looks at Morycus and hugs him dearly. Her face shows a confused look while hugging Morycus while she touches the headband on Morycus head. Maxayus approaches his mother and both Morycus and Maxayus share a group hug with Malaya. Spike jumps off the boat and is greeted by both Rocky and Maya.

“Hey bro!! You made it!" Rocky hugs Spike lifting Spikes feet off the ground. Spike laughs and Rocky gently puts Spike down. Rocky makes way for Maya as both her and Spike share a kiss.

Spike then says. “Your father wanted me to give you, his bracelet."

Spike removes the bracelet from his wrist and hands it to Maya. Maya excitedly says. “Really? I have not asked him for this since I was a young girl."

Maya puts the bracelet on and continues to say. “He must want me to have it now that I am of age."

“This is a way of him expressing how proud he is of you all. I saw he handed Einsberg the coral necklace for Maxayus and Morycus wears his headband."

Spike points out. Maya rubs her bracelet and seems concerned.

Spike asks. “What’s wrong my love?"

Maya chuckles. “Oh, it’s nothing my love come let’s go and explore our new home."

Maya grabs Spikes’ hand and Rocky walks towards Einsberg. While walking towards Einsberg, Raymond bumps into Rocky unintentionally.

Rocky says. “Watch it number guy! You can say excuse me!"

Raymond does not acknowledge and continues to walk.

Einsberg says to Rocky. “Ahh don’t worry about him he’s been acting strange since we got on this boat."

“He needs to be happy, now that he’s reunited with his family." Rocky adds.

Einsberg smiles and speaks. “So, what’s up? You wanted to ask me something?"

Rocky responds. “Yea, listen to be honest with you everyone is reunited with their family and all, I was just wondering if now that I’m not needed here, I can ride back with you? To get the others?"

Einsberg nods his head and replies. “You know what? Yea why not it’s better I’m not riding back alone, at least now I have someone to talk with on the way to get the others."

Rocky smiles and speaks. “Alright, let me tell Spike."

Rocky yells out to Spike. Einsberg laughs and looks around at everyone reuniting with their family. He smiles and sees Shannon with Stacey, he waves at both the ladies and hears Rocky hop on the boat.

“Ok I already untied the boat, whenever you’re ready!"

Einsberg laughs and speaks. “I’m ready, let’s go get the last bunch."

Einsberg turns the boat west and heads towards the open water.

Some children approach Shannon and Stacey and begin to say. “Miss Shannon, Miss Stacey, come quick!! We found something odd."

Shannon and Stacey stare at each other and follow the children towards the odd discovery they’ve made. Stacey and Shannon follow the children and see another group of children cheering on. There, Stacey, and Shannon see one of the hybrid children pulling on the tanto stuck in the bark of an oak tree.

Shannon says. “Children, relax now let me take a look at this, please."

Shannon approaches the Tanto with the red ribbon, Shannon reads the ribbon and sees the writing. “To the future of this city."

Then Shannon begins to pull on the Tanto, the children begin to cheer on Shannon. Shannon pulls and pulls, Stacey comes in to help, both women pull, Shannon then puts her right foot on the tree and Stacey says. "On three!"

The children all count along with the ladies. "One.... Two...... Three!!!!" The ladies pull with all their strength, and both fall back into the ground. All the children laugh and Stacey and Shannon smiled.

Shannon has the tanto in her hand and the piece oak bark attached to it. The ladies and children all look towards the oak tree and see a big hole in the tree. Stacey and Shannon look at each other and nod in agreement to look inside the tree. As both women approach Shannon sees the bottle, she grabs the bottle and sees the scroll inside.

Shannon and Stacey both stare in confusion. "What is it!!" Shouts a child.

Shannon opens the bottle and turns it upside down to reveal the scroll. Both Shannon and Stacey begin to read the scroll aloud to the children.

We then see Raymond walking into the forest wearing an old blanket that was brought from the soldier hybrids. He wears it over his body, Raymond feels someone around. He turns around and sees nothing and only hears birds cawing.

He turns around again and hears Lunas voice. "If you're trying to be discreet it's definitely working."

Raymond stops and does not turn around.

Luna then says. "So, you did it right? You got your memory back?"

Raymond still under the blanket does not respond.

Luna holding her stomach says. "At least tell me your name! I have the right to know that don't I?"

Raymond turns slightly around and speaks. "Raymond, Raymond Styke."

Luna says nothing. Raymond pauses for a while, turns his head, and begins to walk towards the forest again.

"Luowl!!!" Luna shouts.

Raymond stops again and slightly turns his face.

Luna replies. "That's going to be his name."

Luna rubs her belly and speaks. "Luanna, that's going to be her name."

Raymond completely turns around and locks eyes with Luna. Lunas eyes are full of tears as she rubs her belly still.

Raymond approaches Luna puts his hand on her belly and speaks. "Luowl, is going to be the best son ever, you are going to be the greatest mother in the world."

Luna smiles and cries. "What makes you say it's Luowl?"

Raymond smiles and speaks. "I've known it's been a boy this whole time."

Luna cries and caresses Raymond's face. Raymond holds Lunas hand, kisses her hand then turns away. Raymond runs into the forest and vanishes into the woods.

Luna with tears in her eyes while rubbing her belly says. "Good luck, Raymond Styke."

Back at the other side of the forest, Spike sits with Maya and Malaya near a big stone. Morycus is trying to catch fish on the shoreline while Maxayus has already gathered squirrels to feast on.

Shannon and Stacey approach Spike. "Spike, read this."

Shannon hands Spike the letter; Spike reads everything for about two minutes. He stares back at the ladies with a concerned look.

Shannon says. "What do you think?"

Spike then replies. "I think this is our way in; this has all the information we need to reveal ourselves. It's like a call for help and we are the ones who answered. There is enough information here to meet up with the mayor and show him we have a cure."

Stacey and Shannon both smiled.

Shannon then says. "Spike you're going to love this."

Shannon shows Spike the tanto knife with the red ribbon. "This was attached to the letter when we found it Spike."

Spike reads the words. "To the future of this city." Spike holds the tanto and stands up in disbelief.

Spike then says. "God is great, my god is great."

Spike falls to his knees while holding the tanto. Shannon and Stacey tear up and smile.

Maya asks. "What's it says my love?" Spike reads the letter aloud and after reading it, Maya hugs Spike. Malaya folds her palms and prays.

Spike then tells the woman. "Once Einsberg gets back with Ryan and Janjii. We can show him our discovery, then we can finally do our part in saving this planet from this god forsaken disease."

Spike stares at the tanto with the ribbon and the scene pans above the city which looks like it is many miles away. The scene then zooms in fast into the city across the streets and into the buildings. We then see a building window as the scene begins to slow down with the zoom in.

There inside the window on the top building we see a hospital room, inside that hospital room is none other than Ronald Brim, who sits next to his sick daughter Rhonda. Just outside the hospital room, is three men who carry samurai swords wearing all black. Down the hall we see another man with a samurai sword and down the other side a second man holding a samurai sword. The scene then pans out to the ocean view where we can see Einsberg and Rocky heading towards the island. The scene continues west in an unknown location. We see Theodore and Sgt. Luther going over what looks like a map, alongside Hubert and his team. The scene then pans out again and ends in Straton city with Raymond in the back of a small box truck, the box truck driver is unaware of Raymond in the back and looks like he is heading outside of the city. The scene makes one final zoom up into the sky.

Chapter 25:

A Void

Einsberg speeds the boat straight towards the island. Rocky stands next to Henry as both men stare ahead for the last trip before their new lives.

The wind blows through both Einsbergs and Rocky's faces, Einsberg tells Rocky while pointing his finger and smiling. "You see that? There it is land!"

Rocky smiles and Einsberg pats Rocky's back, after two and a half hours they are finally just minutes away from the island. Back on the island, Ryan rests while Reedriake awaits the boat inside the hut with Ryan.

Ryan stretches his body and speaks. "Ahhhh man I so tired right now where is Janjii?"

"He's outside gathering some fish for you while you rest." Reedriake replies.

Ryan laughs and responds. "Man, I love Janjii, he is so thoughtful, are you excited about the city Reedriake?"

Reedriake turns and stares at Ryan seriously.

Ryan then says. "Ok then, sorry I asked."

Reedriake turns back around and continues sharpening his knife. Ryan lays back down on his bed, he closes his eyes for a while then feels as though someone is watching him. Ryan opens his eyes and looks around the room, he notices Reedriake is gone. Ryan lays down again, but this time Reedriake is standing over him. Ryan opens his eyes and looks confused, before Ryan says anything, Reedriake quickly starts to strangle Ryan. Ryan tries to scream for help but can't, Ryan tries to grab Reed's wrist to get his hands off his neck but is too weak to do so. After a while of Reedriake strangling. Ryan starts to turn pale, his eyes grow wide and red, he looks at Reedriake with a look of anger. Reedriake keeps strangling until Ryan's hands grow loose and fall to the to the side letting go of Reedriakes wrist. Ryan is now dead in the hands of Reedriake. Reedriake puts the sheets on Ryan's body and closes his eyes with his fingers.

Reedriake then puts Ryan's body in a sleeping position as though it looks like he is still resting. Reedriake stares at Ryan's body and walks out of the hut with his knife in hand. Reedriake steps out and notices Janjii out in the water looking for fish. Reedriake begins to walk towards Janjii with the knife in hand as he gets closer. He notices ahead of Janjii the boat has arrived. Reedriake quickly puts his knife away and runs back towards the hut where Ryan lays. Einsberg and Rocky see Janjii and shout. Janjii looks up and sees the men approaching, Janjii smiles and waves his arms. It became foggy, so Janjii steps out of the water to make room for the men to dock. Einsberg hops off the boat and Rocky follows.

Janjii says to Rocky. “How did my daughter and wife arrive at their new location my son?"

“Everyone was excited and happy Janjii, I’m sure they can’t wait to see you." Rocky replies.

Janjii looks at Einsberg and speaks. “What about Maxayus sir Einsberg, did you give him the necklace?”

Einsberg holds the necklace in his palm and speaks. “I gave it to him Janjii, then I found it hanging on the steering wheel of the boat on my way here."

Janjii grabs the necklace and smiles sadly.

Einsberg puts his hand on Janjiis shoulder and speaks. “Hey, it’s alright, we’ll talk to him when we get back, you know how these youngsters are, come on now let’s get Ryan."

Janjii and Einsberg walk towards the hut, Reedriake comes out before they can enter.

Einsberg says. “Hey Reedriake, how’s Sir Ryan doing?"

Reedriake smiles and speaks. “He took some of those medicines a while ago, all I heard was Mr. Ryan snoring."

Einsberg and Janjii smile at each other.

Reedriake then says. “Would you like me to wake him Sir Einsberg?"

Henry nods his head and speaks. “That won’t be necessary, he still laying on the stretcher we made for him?"

“Yes, would you like us to carry him to the boat?" Reedriake suggests.

“Sure, I’ll ask Rocky to help you carry him on board." Says Einsberg.

Reedriake looks at Einsberg with a serious look and speaks. "Rocky?"

"Yes, he decided to accompany me on the way here, thank goodness too because I really needed someone to talk with on the way here." Einsberg replies.

Reedriake stares at Henry for a while then snaps out of his head and replies. "Yes, please have Rocky meet me in the hut so we can carry Sir Ryan onto the boat."

Einsberg calls Rocky over and tells him to help Reedriake carry Ryan onto the boat. Ryan lays on a big palm leaf stretcher, Rocky and Reedriake both walk into the hut.

Rocky says. "Oh man, he's out."

Reedriake lifts the side with Ryan's head and Rocky lifts the side with Ryan's feet. Einsberg helps Janjii climb into the boat, Reedriake and Rocky approach the boat holding Ryan's body. Rocky and Reedriake lift the body up while Janjii and Einsberg extend their arms to lift Ryan's body onto the boat.

"Man, that medicine really put him out!" Says Henry.

"Indeed." Replies Janjii.

Janjii rubs his chin while Rocky climbs up the boat. Rocky and Einsberg carry Ryan's body onto the boat's deck room. Janjii helps Reedriake climb aboard, then Einsberg begins to depart from the island. The four men begin to head towards the city.

Reedriake then says. "I'll stay with Sir Ryan, let us know when we get close in case, I have to wake him!"

"Ok, sounds good thank you Reedriake." Einsberg replies.

The day turns into night; the men are already two hours and thirty minutes into the sea. Janjii stands outside the deck, staring into the sea. Janjii holds the coral necklace on the side of his hip.

It begins to rain and Einsberg screams out to Reedriake. "Hey Reedriake, I see land, wake Ryan up we're almost there!"

Janjii heads inside the deck room but does not see Reedriake, he looks at Ryan and speaks. "Sir Ryan please wake up; we are almost home."

Ryan's arm falls lifeless off the stretcher Janjii steps back and realizes Ryan's dead.

Janjii yells out. "Einsberg!!! Something is wrong with Sir Ryan!"

Lightning interrupted some of Janjiis yelling.

Einsberg with Rocky next to him yells out. "What!! I could not hear you!! Is Ryan awake!"

Janjii walks outside the deck room to let Einsberg know what has happened. But just as soon as he walks outside Reedriake stands in front of Janjii and stabs him in the stomach. Janjii looks down as Reedriake twists the knife into Janjiis Stomach. Janjii grabs Reedriake by the throat, but Reedriake forces himself with the knife still inside Janjii towards the railing of the boat. Janjiis back is on the railing Reedriake pulls out the knife from Janjiis stomach and holds it across Janjiis neck. During this moment Rocky walks towards the deck and sees Reedriake with Janjii holding the knife towards his neck.

Rocky yells at Reedriake. "Hey!! What are you doing asshole!!"

Reedriake looks at Rocky and quickly slices the knife across Janjiis neck. Reedriake grabs the coral necklace quickly from Janjiis hip and tosses Janjiis body overboard. Rocky tackles Reedriake and both begin to tussle on the boats wet floor. When Rocky tackled Reedriake he knocked the knife off his hand. Rocky being stronger than Reedriake ends up on top of Reedriake, Rocky begins to punch Reedriake in the face. Einsberg is trying to see what all the commotions about and is not concentrating on what is ahead. The boat loses a bit of control and as Rocky tries to land another punch on Reedriake, he gets slammed against the side of the railing due to the boat's movement. Reedriake then stands up and runs towards his knife, Rocky chases right behind Reedriake. The boat moves again this time Rocky falls on his face while Reedriake holds onto the railing. Reedriake manages to reach for his knife on the wet deck, but when he turns around Rocky tackles him again. Rocky is on top of Reedriake again, this time he is trying to impale Reedriakes face with Reedriakes own knife, while Reedriake still holds his knife. With Rocky's strength he is using Reedriakes own hands to impale the knife in Reedriakes face. The knife is inches away from Reedriakes left eye, then the boat again loses control. The knife slips and slashes Reedriakes left eyebrow but causes Rocky to fall sideways. Reedriake stands up with the coral necklace in his hand, as he runs towards the railing, he puts the necklace around his neck and jumps off the boat and into the water. Rocky runs towards the railing and looks for Reedriake in the water but sees nothing. Einsberg cannot control the winds and rain and with the darkness, Einsberg can't see anything. Then the boat crashes into the stones located on the shore of the forest. The boat crashes and all the hybrids come out to check on everyone on board.

Einsberg yells. "Rocky what happened?!"

"Reedriake that son of a bitch!! He betrayed us all!!"

Maxayus, Spike, Maya, and Morycus all jump on the boat.

Maxayus searches for Janjii he turns to Rocky and yells. "Rocky!! Where is my father!"

Rocky looks at Maxayus with a sad look, he nods his head and begins to cry. "I'm sorry Maxayus, I was too late, Reedriake he.......... he."

"What did Reedriake do Rocky! What!"

Maxayus grabs Rocky and demands an answer.

Rocky looks at Maxayus with tears in his eyes and speaks. "He killed him, Reedriake killed Janjii and tossed him overboard."

Maxayus releases Rocky and walks away in shock, Maxayus stops and turns back towards

Rocky and speaks. "The necklace, Where's the necklace Rocky!"

"That son of a bitch took it from Janjii and jumped off the boat!!" Rocky sobs.

Maxayus drops to his knees and begins to cry. Morycus breaks down as well, Spike holds Maya while she cries on Spikes' shoulders hysterically. Einsberg heads to the deck room only to see Ryan's body thrown around like a rag doll. Einsberg turns the body over and checks for a pulse, Einsberg gets no pulse and at once begins to cry.

"Ah shit brother, shit, please brother come back............ come back!!" Einsberg cries on Ryan's lifeless chest.

Shannon and Stacey climbed onto the boat and head towards the deck room; there they see Henry on Ryan's body crying hysterically. The women all look at Henry in shock. Henry looks at both Shannon and Stacey and cries out.

"He's gone!! He's gone!!......... there wasn't anything......... it's my fault, I'm sorry, it's my fault!!"

Shannon and Stacey drop to their knees, and both women begin to cry hysterically together. After a couple of minutes of mourning Spike, Maxayus, Maya, Rocky and Morycus hop off the boat first. They are awaited by some hybrids on ground; Malaya is ahead of those hybrids. Maya looks at her mother, both women stare at each other, Maya nods her head and begins to cry while hugging Malaya. Behind them is Einsberg, Stacey and Shannon, Einsberg carries Ryan's dead body and jumps off the boat with the help of Rocky and Spike. The rain hits everyone hard in this sad and horrible moment, Ryan and Janjii are dead. The one responsible is nowhere to be found, Spike looks around at everyone's sad faces in the middle of the rain.

Spike looks up towards the rainy sky and speaks. "Heavenly Father, in the midst of this difficult time, we come to you with heavy hearts, seeking your comfort and strength. We feel the weight of this unfortunate event, and we ask for your grace to guide us through the pain and uncertainty. Please grant us peace in our minds and hearts, and remind us that even in darkness, your love shines brightly. Help us to find hope in your promises, and to trust in your plan, even when we cannot understand it. We surrender this situation to you and ask for your healing touch on our spirits. In Jesus' name, Amen."

Spike puts his head back down and falls to his knees crying. The scene pans out as the night sky remains gray and the darkness remains silent.

Chapter 26:

Hope……

The hybrids continue to help one another settle in as daylight hits the forest. Einsberg is sitting in front of a fire with a roasted squirrel on a stick. He looks like he hasn't slept all day and is still shaken up by the crash. Spike walks out of his hut looking around and sees Henry sitting down, Spike decides to walk over and sit across Einsberg. Henry doesn't acknowledge Spike and continues to eat the roasted squirrel. Spike stares at Henry with both his elbows on his thighs, awaiting Henry to speak.

Spike breaks the silence and speaks. "I didn't sleep last night, Maya is so exhausted from crying, I think she forced herself to sleep."

Henry continues to eat and says nothing; he doesn't even look at Spike.

Spike takes a deep breath. "Eins... the plan, we need to discuss a new plan."

Einsberg throws the half-eaten squirrel on the ground and yells. "There is no plan!!!"

Spike stares at Henry while sitting down.

Henry then says. "Can't you see we lost loved ones, there is no more hope, we all give up." Henry Sobs. He continues by saying. "This was a bad idea and it's all my fault, I say we live here and just let the world go-"

"Then what!! Henry!! We wait here and die!! Janjii and Ryan lost their lives, and you want to give up!!! The hell with that! We did not come all this way for you to lose your faith!!!" Spike yells.

Shannon hears Spike screaming and walks over to listen. Some of the other hybrids gather around to listen as well.

Spike continues. "Ryan and Janjii didn't die for nothing, and we need to make sure of that. They would want us to continue with our plan, now we have to make a new one."

Einsberg puts his head down and agrees. "What do we do Spike? What do you suggest?"

Spike tosses the scroll with the letter written by Ronald inside to Einsberg, Shannon watches Einsberg read it.

Henry's eyes grow wide. "What...... how did you find this?" Einsberg asks.

Spike replies. "It's a call for help left in these woods; this is our new plan."

"I.... I don't understand. What are you planning to do Spike?" Henry questioned.

"You have those capsules for the cure still, correct?" Spike asks.

Henry looks at Shannon, which she is already holding in the backpack. Henry grabs the backpack slowly and stares at Shannon.

Spike continues to speak. “I need you to come with me to the hospital, Shannon has already agreed, but I need you to join us as well."

Einsberg asks. “Why me Spike, I have lost all hope."

Spike walks towards Einsberg inches from his face and speaks. “Because you are the hope for all of us, you were the one who migrated all the hybrids, now you will be the one to bring us into this world."

Einsberg looks around and sees hybrids gathered around watching him, Henry looks inside his backpack and pulls out a capsule. Henry closes his eyes and tears run down his face; he looks at Spike and nods his head. Spike extends his arms and both Henry and Spike hug each other. Shannon cries while Henry breaks down emotionally on Spike.

Henry says. “You are a warrior at heart and in soul, I appreciate you, I love you, thank you for giving me strength."

“I love you too Henry, now let us get your life back and let’s honor those who aren’t with us, let’s give everyone hope again. Today we cure everyone’s spirits across the globe." Spike says while holding Henry tightly.

Moments after Spikes speech, Shannon and Henry gather some army clothes scavenged in the wreck. Shannon finds a uniform and begins to change, on the other side of the boat’s wreck, Einsberg looks over at Shannon and walks towards her, Einsberg holds his uniform in hand.

Henry clears his throat while Shannon undresses. “May I come in?" Einsberg says jokingly.

Shannon smiles and responds. “You may."

Einsberg rubs Shannon's shoulders and begins to kiss her neck, Shannon smiles with her eyes closed and speaks. "You're still going to love me?"

Einsberg backs up and turns Shannon around while holding her chin and speaks. "Of course I'll still love you, why would you think that?"

"Well, we aren't on the island anymore Henry, we are going back to reality, back to society. I just want to be sure this isn't a fantasy we had on the island." Shannon explains.

Einsberg holds Shannon close and speaks. "I don't need an island to tell me how I feel about you. I want to spend the rest of my life with you."

Shannon smiles and both share a very passionate and romantic kiss.

Back in the forest Spike gets ready to head to the hospital along with the doctors, he walks in a half-built hut that's still missing half a rooftop. In the hut Maya lays in a bed of leaves, she turns her body and sees Spike standing and looking towards her. "I'll be heading out with the Doctors my love, I.... I'm sorry for everything you are going through."

Spike is about to walk out of the hut, but Maya grabs Spikes' arm. "My love, I will regain my strength, I will be back to my old self. But I tell you this, if I lose you, I will never be the same." Maya says.

Spike turns towards Maya and gives her a big hug while slightly pulling her up from the leaf bed.

Spike says to Maya. "I will return to you my love, along with a new beginning followed."

Spike kisses Maya's hand and heads out the hut. Spike is walking towards the hut where Shannon and Einsberg wait. During this walk Spike sees Maxayus, who is sitting on a stone facing the forest trees, which have sunlight beaming through the trees. Maxayus turns slightly and sees Spike, Spike nods his head to greet Maxayus.

Maxayus stands up and walks towards Spike, Spike stands still waiting for Maxayus to speak. "Spike, I want to thank you brother, you really said some inspiring words moments ago."

Spike nods his head in acceptance. Maxayus stares at Spike and speaks. "He knew he wasn't going to make it you know. The things he was saying, the way he was acting, he knew.......... I...... I also knew."

Maxayus begins to break down in tears. "I did nothing to help him, I did nothing to prevent his demise, yet I complained and grew angrier. I grew angry because I did not know how to stop what was going to happen." Am I wrong brother? Will I be punished for my sins?"

"No sin was committed here Maxayus, I do not feel as though you should apologize. I do feel though, however, that your father, our chief, did have an intuition. He did the best he could in trying to say goodbyes before his soul departed. But brother, you did nothing wrong in acting in the way you did. You felt scared and confused knowing that someone you love, admire, and adore was leaving us. But you, though we may not look like it. You are human, you have feelings, you have emotions and all those things are what makes you human. God has called upon your father, like he would call upon us one day. Do not feel guilt, rather share Janjiis wisdom, his ways, everything he has taught you, share them with your future children and continue your generation through his ways. That's how you as his son will repay your father."

Maxayus stares at Spike with teary eyes, he composes himself and speaks. "I heard you were good with your words brother, I'm glad I had the pleasure to listen to them in firsthand."

Maxayus turns around and begins to walk back towards the stone he was sitting on. Spike watches Maxayus for a quick moment and continues to walk towards Einsberg and Shannon's hut. Morycus is behind a tree with Janjiis headband in his hand, Spike notices and immediately changes his direction towards Morycus. Rocky stands right across Morycus who was comforting his friend beforehand. Spike walks over and hugs both men.

Morycus begins to cry on Spikes shoulder, Spike rubs Morycus back and faces Morycus while keeping his hand on Morycus shoulders. "You have to be strong Morycus, though you are the youngest your family needs you more than ever."

"But why me Spike, I don't understand how I can be the one that holds this family together?"

Spike smiles and replies. "You are the youngest of your siblings, you have seen it all in your family. You, being the youngest, have watched your brother grow, you have watched Maya grow and you watched both your parents instruct your brother and sister ways that you were taught soon.

You Morycus have always been a step closer than your siblings, this is why they need you the most because you, out of all your siblings, you have been the most observant, most curious, and most caring for this family. Now you must be the one that upholds everyone by using just those things I mentioned to you but use it as a tool to help your mother and siblings, they don't have those tools, only you can possess them. Remember be yourself and follow who you want to be in the process of healing my brother."

Morycus smiles. "Thank you, brother Spike, thank you."

Spike rubs Morycus' head and shakes Rocky's hand. Spike then continues his walk towards the doctor's hut. Rocky and Morycus stare at Spike as he walks away.

Morycus says to Rocky. "You are lucky he is kin of yours Rocky, his energy is really vibrant and positive."

“Yea that’s my bro, without him I wouldn’t be who I am, without his words, I wouldn’t have the strength to deal with my thoughts and emotions." Rocky says.

“I can see him being a chief, a leader for our people." Morycus says.

Rocky smiles and agrees with Morycus. “To be honest Rocky, I feel like he just recruited me for some odd reason."

“Well consider yourself his left-hand man then little bro, which is one person you want to serve. Because that guy there serves God and if he just made you feel that way, then it’s probably one hundred percent accurate." Rocky responds.

Spike finally approaches the hut, Henry and Shannon Walk out wearing soldier uniforms. All three stared at each other and nodded. Einsberg holds Shannon’s hand, he then extends his other hand and holds Spikes’ right hand.

Spike closes his eyes, but right before he prays Einsberg says. “Spike, if you don’t mind, may I do the honor?"

Spike smiles and speaks. “Of course."

All three hold hands and bow their heads as Einsberg begins to pray. “Lord, I pray that the storm from this change be removed. But if it's Your will for me to walk through it, I thank You that You go with me. Thank you also for raising good things from impossible circumstances. No matter what happens, I trust you to see me all the way through....... Amen."

The three all say Amen and continue to walk together through the trees, we see the scene pans upwards, where a clear view of Straton City is shown, as the path of our beloved characters head towards this city, on this powerful and unforgettable morning.

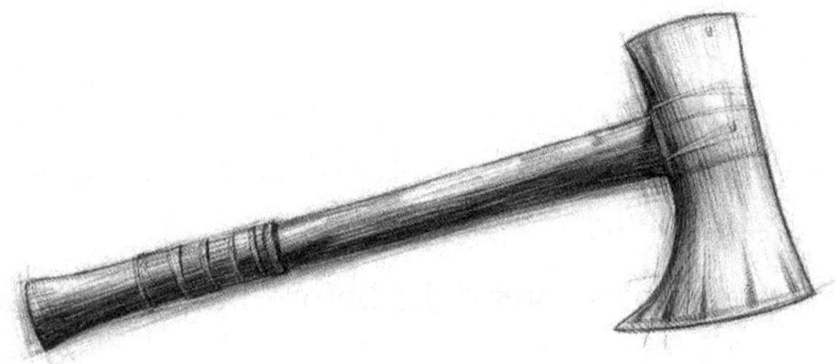

Chapter 27:

Reserved

A military helicopter flies over an open ocean; the helicopter is heading straight towards the island where the hybrids were found. The helicopter reaches the island and hovers over for about a minute or two. The helicopter is carrying a ten-foot aluminum crate, with what looks like holes on the side containing an animal of some sort. The helicopter drops smoke gases on the island making the island foggy and blind. The helicopter hovers over the whole island making sure these smoke gases cover the entire area. For another ten minutes the smoke slowly clears, then the helicopter releases the crate, and the crate splits open like a banana peel. Out of the crates we hear snarling and growling, we can't see what it is, but we hear these creatures running through the island's woods, as if they are searching for something. Back at Theodore's exclusive island we see Theodore, Luther, and Hubert along with his team staring at a two screened monitor. On the monitors we can see that whatever was released on the hybrids island is being observed by Theodore and the rest of the men in the room. These creatures have cameras on them and are being monitored by Theodore himself. Theodore watches desperately as these creatures run through the island, searching for what looks like, the hybrids and scientists.

Luther with his arms crossed watching the monitor says. "It looks like they are gone sir."

"Theo, there is nothing there, we would've seen them by now." Hubert adds.

Theodore says nothing and continues to view the monitors. A dispatcher radio calls on Theodore's radio.

The dispatcher says. "Sir, the island is clear, the huts and woods have no sign of life form. Would you like us to keep searching sir?"

Theodore does not reply and the dispatcher continues. "Sir, do you copy? I repeat, there are no signs of life here on this island sir."

Sergeant Luther grabs the radio and responds to the dispatcher. "Copy that soldier, let's come home and tranquillize the HBS experiments and load them back up on the crate."

"Copy that Sergeant, we are on it now!"

Luther puts the radio dispatcher back on the charging station in front of Theodore. Hubert stares at Theodore, Theodore continues to watch the monitors without saying a word.

Hubert puts his hand on Theodore's shoulder and speaks. "Hey Theo, you, ok? Talk to me."

Theodore grabs Hubert's hand and twists it behind Hubert's back, while Theodore stands up and slams Hubert on the table next to him.

Theodore yells. "You insignificant piece of dog shit! Do you realize what is happening right now!"

"Ahhh, Please Theo! Please you are hurting me!!" Hubert pleads.

Theodore continues yelling. "I should blow your damn brains out right now!!"

Theodore grabs his gun from his holster located on his hip; Theodore puts the barrel of his gun behind Hubert's head while still holding Hubert's wrist behind Hubert's back.

Hubert cry's out. "Theo!! Please do not!! Think about Father!!"

Theodore lets go of Hubert and throws him off the table. Hubert stares at the group of scientists and Theodore ends up shooting Watkins between the eyes. The other scientists scream in horror. Theodore still pointing his gun towards where Watkins used to stand is huffing and puffing. The Sergeant smiles and just observes Theodore. Theodore finally lowers his gun slowly and begins to breathe back normally.

Theodore begins to laugh and speak. "Oh, my I apologize my colleagues, I lost my temper a little there didn't I?"

The two remaining Scientists Timothy Yang and Walter Richardson look in fear and say nothing, they nervously continue with their hands in the air.

Theodore then yells. "I said.... I lost my temper there.... Didn't I!!!!!"

Both Yang and Richardson respond nervously with a "yes."

Theodore then laughs and walks over Carl Watkins dead body; Theodore stands over the body and speaks. "Hubert..."

"Ye... yes Theo?"

"Have Carl Watkins body cremated and out of my sight please, this is because of you... so make yourself useful and dispose of him."

“Yes Theo, right away."

“Oh Hubert, before you go, next bullet is for you and the hell with my promise I made with Father."

Hubert puts his head down in shame and drags Watkins body out the room, with a trail of blood following.

Theodore stares at the other two scientists and speaks. “What are you all still doing in here! Go help Hubert now!!!"

The two scientists ran out of the room in fear. Theodore walks over to his chair and puts his gun inside the drawer; he rubs his forehead and takes a deep breath. The Sergeant sits on the chair across Theodore and awaits Theodore’s orders.

Theodore then says. “What now Sergeant, what now?"

Theodore pulls out a bottle of vodka and then two glasses, he pours each glass, Luther grabs one and Theodore chugs the other.

Luther then says. “They couldn’t have gotten far, my guess and this is just guessing sir, since James’s experiment is with them what if they headed to Straton City?"

Theodore looks at the Sergeant and asks. “What makes you guess that?"

“Well sir, it is only four hours on a boat ride from the island, and it is also where James's creation is from." Luther replies.

Theodore stares at Luther and speaks. “Very well then, let’s give it a try."

“Let’s?" The Sergeant says.

“Yes, Sergeant this time I am joining you on this expedition, not like the last time I let you go at it alone. This time I want to be involved."

The Sergeant smiles and speaks. “I’ll tell Eric to get the chopper ready then, we head out in ten minutes."

Luther runs out of the room. Theodore remains seated and pours himself another glass of vodka, Theodore then throws the glass against the wall and begins to hold the side of his head with both his palms.

Theodore then mumbles. "I swear if they reveal themselves to the world, I am fucked!!"

Theodore phone rings, Theodore stares at it and lets it ring. The phone stops ringing and then rings again after a minute. The scene pans out while we see a stressed Theodore sitting in his chair watching the phone ring and ring and ring.

Straton City……

Back in the City... Henry, Spike and Shannon Walk out of the woods and into the empty streets of Straton City. Henry and Shannon are both dressed in military uniform, while Spike wears an all-black hoodie and black pants with some military boots. Spike walks in between Shannon and Henry; the group also have with them Ronald's letter that he wrote and Einsberg carries his backpack on him. It takes the group about twenty minutes until they finally arrive at Straton City Hospital. There the group can see the hospital has people in front camping out, some people are begging and pleading with front door security to be let in, others look like they have gone insane just laughing and talking to themselves on the sidewalk. Einsberg and Shannon stare at each-other in shame. The group approached front door security. The security salutes the group and lets them walk right in, if the outside of the hospital looked bad, nothing compares to the inside lobby. It is a mess, papers thrown on the floor, people's medical records in the trash and the place smells like a urinal. Henry, Spike and Shannon Walk slowly across the crowd to the receptionist desk, on the way to the desk, Spike sees a little girl by herself crying next to what looks like her mother's lifeless body. He then sees an old man holding a baby, who looks no older than six months, the old man is crying in the baby's lifeless body.

Spike turns his head away and begins to think to himself. "Father lord I beg you, guide me with all your strength to restore faith within the people."

The group finally make it to the receptionist desk; a stressed looking woman hands the group some paperwork to fill out.

Shannon then clears her throat; the receptionist looks over and speaks. "My apologies soldier I'm so use to handing paperwork I didn't notice who was in front of me, how may I assist you?"

Henry says. "We'd like to speak with Ronald Brim please."

The receptionist stares at the group with an odd look; she picks up the personal phone she carries and makes a call.

She says on the phone. "Soldiers are asking for Ronald."

She stares at the group for a while then responds on the phone. "Very well, ok I'll tell them."

The receptionist hangs up the phone and asks. "May I get your badges please?"

Einsberg and Shannon stare at each other and begin to pat on their own body as if they are looking for something.

Einsberg smiles and speaks. "We must have left them back at base." The receptionist is not having it.

She speaks. "Well sorry without your badges, I can't let you in."

Henry walks close to the reception desk and whispers. "Please it's very important, listen we know the room number, just let his security come down here and escort us to him."

"Yea, which is not going to happen. I just got on the phone with security, and he says Ronald does not have a meeting today with any soldiers. So, either you leave or I'll make you leave myself."

The receptionist then pulls out a Glock and sets it right in front of her.

Einsberg then says. “Please listen, we can save his daughter-"

Einsberg takes his backpack off and the receptionist draws her gun at Einsberg. “I’m warning you!! Put the backpack down!! Nobody is getting past this lobby you hear me!!"

Spike stares at Shannon and Shannon stared back at Spike.

Spike says. “I’m going." The receptionist stared at Spike while still pointing her gun at Einsberg and spoke. “The hell you aren’t!"

Einsberg tosses the backpack to Spike and Spike grabs the letter from Shannon. Spike quickly runs towards the elevators. The receptionist jumps over the desk and begins to fire at Spike; Shannon jumps on the receptionist while Einsberg grabs her gun. Spike removes the boots and continues to run down the hallway.

Einsberg yells echoing down the hallway as he screams. “Go Spike!!! Gooooooo!!!!"

Chapter 28:

It all goes down

Spike runs down the Hallway with the backpack on his back and the letter in his pocket.

Another security guard sees Spike, gets on his personal phone, and speaks. "Bodyguards we have an intruder heading towards the mayor I repeat the mayor is in danger."

Back in the hospital room where Ronald sits side by side with his wife Wilma and his daughter lays on the hospital bed, one of his bodyguards knocks on the door.

Ronald stands up and answers, the bodyguard says to Ronald. "Sir, we have a situation."

Ronald closes the door behind him and stands outside with his bodyguard, Ronald asks. “What’s going on?"

The scene then changes and we see Spike still running down the long hallway, Spike pushes the elevator buttons to the fourth floor, the elevator doors open and its four bodyguards carrying samurai swords coming out. The first bodyguard without hesitation swings his samurai sword at Spike, Spike does a back flip avoiding the swing and begins to run towards the hospital’s stairwell. The four bodyguards run after Spike shouting with their samurai swords in hand. Spike begins to head up the stairway. The bodyguards run right behind him and now, there are bodyguards running down towards Spike. Spike quickly climbs using the railing of the stairs, which causes him to skip through the guards coming down, some of the bodyguards swing their swords in a desperate attempt to wound Spike. Spike then enters through the second-floor door jumping over a guard, who was waiting and begins to run at him. Spike then slides through another guard’s legs who was behind the first guard. Spike heads towards the elevator doors from the second floor; he quickly pushes the button to the fourth floor but this time the doors do not open.

We can hear the guards radio going off as one says. “Maintenance has shut down the elevator."

Spike notices the elevator is not working, he opens the elevator doors with both his hands using all his strength, he then climbs the elevator’s cable to the third floor. Spike jumps to the door of the third floor from inside the elevator’s cable, he opens it with both hands. As he jumps into the third floor, Spike sees three of the mayor’s bodyguards, with nun chucks in their hands. Spike takes a deep breath, and the bodyguards come charging at Spike. Spike jumps in the air doing a split kick, kicking two of them in the face. The final guard standing, begins to move the nun chucks around, running towards Spike. The guard swings the nun chucks trying to hit Spike while running towards him. Spike bobs and weaves dodging the chucks as he moves to the side. Spike cartwheels to the left kicking the bodyguard on his shoulder, the bodyguard almost falls into the open elevator shaft, but Spike grabs the back of his shirt and tosses him to the side. Spike continues to run through the hallway, towards the stairwell that will lead him to the fourth floor. As Spike continues to run, the bodyguard Spike tossed to the side calls for backup on his radio.

Inside room 411 Ronald's bodyguard who warned about an intruder gets the call for backup.

Ronald stares at his guard and the bodyguard says. "Sir we must evacuate immediately."

"No!!! Leave me, I will not leave my family's side.... I .... I don't care anymore, I just want to be here with my little girl, during her last moments."

The guard nods his head and speaks. "Then you be with her sir, we will protect this room and die trying."

In the stairwell Spike makes it through the fourth floor, as soon as he walks on the fourth floor from the stairwell, the whole hallway is dark. Spike is breathing fast and quickly begins to breathe slow, Spike slowly walks towards the hallway and hears a whiff sound from behind him. Spike feels one of the capsules break from inside the backpack and realizes the backpack has been hit by a ninja star. Spike quickly begins to run in zig zag, while the ninja stars fly across room. Still in the dark there are bodyguards in front of Spike, Spike dodges all the bodyguards like he is running a football field to score. Spike runs along the walls, pushes and kicks through bodyguards without hurting them too badly, just enough to make them fall or stumble. But as he approaches room 411, he sees four men come out with swords in their hands. They lock eyes with Spike, the men put on what looks like samurai masks over their mouth. Spike waits for the men to make a move, the men all charge at him screaming, Spike does a backwards cartwheel and jumps from left to right, off the wall towards the men.

The men pause for a second...Spike gets closer, they start swinging their swords at Spike. Spike limbos through one sword and trips the man with his foot. He dodges another swing that almost cuts Spikes head off and punches the man quickly in the nose. The other two swordsmen charge at Spike as he runs into a room. In the room the patients scream in horror, the two swordsmen continue to swing their swords at Spike. Spike grabs a coffee mug in the room and breaks it on one of the swordsmen's head. Spike then grabs a blanket from the patients' bed and tosses it to the other swordsmen. The man removes the blanket from his face and Spike drop kicks the man out the door. The other men storm into the room with their swords. Spike turns around and sees a window. He breaks open the window and climbs out to the side of the building. With no fear, Spike runs to his left, down two rooms, he breaks that window from the outside as the swordsmen look on. He climbs through the window, startles some patients and heads back towards the hallway where two doors down he sees room 411. The swordsmen see him and run towards Spike, Spike opens the room and heads in locking the door behind him, the men bang the door. Spike sees Ronald and his wife next to their daughter's bed; they don't say a word or even acknowledge Spike. Ronald and his wife just pray with their eyes closed; their daughter breathes through a machine. A nurse who is in the room with both Ronald and Wilma looks at Spike in shock but says nothing. The men scream from the outside.

"Sir, are you OK!!!"

"Let's break this door down!"

"I tried, it's unbreakable!!!"

"I'll get a key then!"

"Hurry!!! Go!!"

In the room Spike breathes heavily, he stares at the mayor. The mayor still not acknowledging Spike says nothing.

Then Ronald Speaks. "If you are here to harm me, there is not much damage to do.... I am already broken enough."

Spike then answers with heavy breathing. "Sir...... I am not...... Here.....to cause......harm...... Listen to me.... I have...... I am..... The cure...."

At this moment, Ronald opens his eyes and stares at Spike. He slowly stands and slowly walks towards Spike, Spike who's back is against the door stares at Ronald.

Ronald says. "What...... Who are you???" Spike goes in his pockets and shows Ronald his own letter he wrote and left in the forest.

Ronald grabs the letter and speaks. "How did you... what..."

Ronald falls on his knees and begins to cry. Spike then takes his backpack off which has a ninja star lunged into it, Spike takes out one of the capsules and speaks. Please sir, we have no time...... my blood is the cure."

Ronald looks at his wife and speaks. "Wilma what do I do?"

Wilma with tears in her eyes replies. "I'm willing to try anything."

Ronald looks at Spike, then the nurse, Ronald grabs the capsule from Spike and hands it to the nurse. The nurse grabs a syringe and draws the liquid from the capsule, the nurse stares at Ronald, Ronald nods his head in agreement. The nurse then looks at Spike, and she injects Rhonda's IV bag with the liquid.

After a couple of minutes, the nurse starts examining Rhonda and speaks. "Temperature is dropping, Saliva is looking normal, Blood is going back to normal, heartbeat at normal movement."

As she continues to read off Rhonda's health. Ronald looks at his daughter and starts crying tears of joy. Wilma hugs Rhonda in her bed also crying, the bodyguards finally open the door and pause. They all look in shock as Rhonda opens her eyes.

Rhonda says. “Mom...Dad."

“My baby!!!! My little girl!!" Ronald cries.

Spike smiles, still breathing heavy and speaks. “Let her rest for about three days, it helps the organs heal back to normal."

“Get him some water!!" Ronald yells.

“You are an Angel sent from heaven." Wilma cries.

Ronald approaches Spike and speaks. “What’s your name?"

Spike breathing fast replies. “Spike....... Spike Jimmy Matthews."

Chapter 29:

Much more than meets the Eye

Ronald walks downstairs with Spike. Alongside Ronald and Spike, Ronald's bodyguards accompany them. As Spike and Ronald make it to the lobby, there Shannon and Einsberg look at Spike while they were being held under arrest by local police officers. Ronald walks over with Spike and tells the police officer to release both Shannon and Henry. The police officer does so, and Shannon runs over to Spike and hugs him. Henry walks slowly towards Spike; both men stare at one another. Henry cries and hugs Spike as well; everyone looks in shock. The people of Straton City gather around, and bodyguards stand by to keep everyone calm. The crowd is very calm, they are silent and whispering, Ronald introduces himself to Shannon and Henry as they all begin to walk outside. The People of Straton City continue to look through the hospital glass door from the inside. Spike turns around and sees the same little girl who was crying in the lobby, with her hand to the glass door. Spike puts his hand on the glass matching hers, the little girl smiles, and Spike smile back. This beautiful moment is suddenly interrupted by loud helicopter blades, which hover over the front of the hospital Entrance. Ronald looks up squinting as the winds of the blades hit his face, Henry stares in anger as he sees who is inside the helicopter.

The Helicopter lands and Theodore hop off clapping his hands while walking towards Ronald. "Hello Mr. Brim, congratulations!"

Ronald stares at Theodore in confusion.

Theodore then continues to speak. "Mr. Brim I would like to personally congratulate you in becoming the first city in the world to receive the cure to the Eyidrotheria disease."

Theodore continues to clap his hands. Ronald stares at Theodore and asks. "Hello Mr.???"

"Ahh Theodore, Theodore Evans, my good man. I am, well in charge and fund this private organization by our government, to discover and develop this new and successful Remedy."

Ronald turns towards Einsberg and Spike and notices they are not in agreement with what Theodore is saying.

Ronald smiles and replies. "Well Mr. Evans, you have a hell of a way to introduce this new Remedy of yours."

Theodore laughs. "Well, I do tend to go overboard with these new discoveries, especially one that is going to restore humanity, don't you think?"

Ronald laughs and crosses his arms and speaks. "So, what can I help you with Mr. Evans?"

"Oh, you've done enough Mr. Brim, I just wanted to showcase to the world, the beginning of a new beginning." Theodore laughs.

Ronald turns around and asks Spike. “Is this true Spike? Is this guy the one responsible for bringing you here?"

Spike doesn’t reply, but stares at Theodore like he is ready to attack him.

Ronald looks back at Theodore and speaks. “I don’t think he likes you very much Mr. Evans, I’ll tell you what.... How about Spike and this fine gentleman and his lovely partner here, stay in my city. Meanwhile you and your Sergeant over there continue to spread the cure across the world."

Theodore stares at Ronald with a sinister look and replies. “Mr. Brim I am not asking, I am simply explaining to you the purpose of this matter, in fact these two scientists here have violated a term of agreement, which they both have with me. Meanwhile this one called Spike is a property of the United States Government."

“No!! He is the son of James Matthews, the man you all murdered three years ago, on an island we refuged to...to escape from you!!!" Einsberg yells.

Sergeant Luther walks in front of Theodore and points his assault rifle at Einsberg. Ronald’s bodyguards all pull out their samurai swords and stand in front of Einsberg.

Theodore smiles and tells Sergeant Luther. “Easy Sergeant, lower your weapon, we have too many witnesses around. Let’s manage this state of matter......legally."

Sergeant Luther lowers his rifle, and both men head back on the helicopter. Theodore says. “Well Mr. Brim, I’m sorry this had to go another route, you will be getting a call from my attorneys."

“I’ll be waiting Mr. Evans." Ronald replies.

The men stare at Ronald as the helicopter's blades begin to spin and the helicopter hovers over the city, the men fly off towards the east side of the city. We then see Theodore and Luther in the helicopter looking down on the city's forest while flying east.

Theodore's eyes widen as he yells at the pilot. "Pilot!! Land, Land the chopper now!"

"What's going on sir?" Asks Luther.

Theodore points to the ground and Luther gets his rifle ready. Luther looks through the rifles' scope and smiles.

Luther then tells the pilot. "Hey land in front of him."

The chopper lands onto a strip of dirt which is located right outside the forest area. Both Luther and Theodore hop off the helicopter and run towards a figure, who is walking along the strip.

Theodore looks at Luther and speaks. "It's a hybrid shoot him!" Luther smiles and speaks. "No sir, trust me on this one."

"What in the hell are you talking about Sergeant this is an order." Theodore yells.

Luther smiles and speaks. "Sir, believe me this one is good."

Theodore looks at Luther and speaks. "Oh, and how do you know of this?"

"Well sir, let's just say I sort of made a deal with this one, isn't that right hybrid!"

The hybrid looks at Sergeant Luther, we see it is Reedriake he is talking to. Reedriake survived the crash with a scar on his right eye and wearing the blue coral necklace. Reedriake looks over to Theodore and Luther while he Smiles.

Back inside the woods

Spike walks with Ronald, Shannon and Henry Walk behind the two, Ronald says. "The last time I came this deep into the woods was the day I wrote that letter you all found."

Spike stops Ronald and speaks. "Wait here Sir."

Ronald stops while Spike goes deeper into the woods, Ronald turns to look at Shannon and Einsberg, both stand awaiting on Spike. Ronald then hears twigs breaking from all around. Ronald's eyes grow wide as he looks around in disbelief, he falls on his behind unable to hold his balance, as Ronald sees his entire surrounding, we can see the forest fills with hybrids. Female, children, and males just looking at him up in the trees and from the ground.

Ronald gasps and speaks. "My god."

Spike comes out from the trees and walks towards Ronald.

"Sir.... These are my people; they are................ the Remedy."

Ronald looks around in disbelief and in awe, as a new chapter will begin between hybrids and humans.

The End…

Coming Soon..................

Books By: J.Z. Elazar

(I)The Book of Mathis

(VI) Remedy: Queued Hope

www.ingramcontent.com/pod-product-compliance
Lightning Source LLC
LaVergne TN
LVHW081324110826
845149LV00007B/1582

* 9 7 9 8 9 9 1 8 8 5 5 4 6 *